"Terry, I'd die . . . I'd just wither up and die back on a farm."

"No, you wouldn't, Julie." He gently turned her face back to his. "Not if you loved me. Not with God's help."

She looked up at him then—at that beautiful tender mouth, forever begging for a kiss. More than anything else in the world, she wanted to give it to him.

But to spend the rest of her life on a farm? She didn't think she could love *any* man that much!

THE
DISGUISE OF
LOVE

Mary LaPietra

BOOKS

of the Zondervan Publishing House
Grand Rapids, Michigan

THE DISGUISE OF LOVE
Copyright © 1985 by The Zondervan Corporation
1415 Lake Drive, S.E.
Grand Rapids, Michigan

ISBN 0-310-46812-4

Edited by Nancye Willis
Series Editor: Anne Severance
Designed by Kim Koning

Printed in the United States of America

85 86 87 88 89 90 91 / 10 9 8 7 6 5 4 3 2 1

*To all dedicated policemen
—whatever their dreams—
and all the women who
love them.*

CHAPTER 1

WITH THE LIBRARY CLOSED SIGN still up on one of the big double doors of the old mansion, Julie stormed down the stone steps and through the wrought-iron gate. She then swung right, heading for the police station four blocks away.

Heedless of the curious heads that turned in her direction, she adjusted her pink cashmere tam. Most of the people on the sidewalk that crisp March morning knew Julie Chambers—the petite and always-smiling dark-haired, dark-eyed young woman who usually could be found behind the desk at the Midtown Branch Library.

But this was a Julie was one none of them had ever seen before: Her brown eyes anything but smiling; her small chin thrust out in determination; her open navy peacoat and pleated tartan skirt flared in the wake of emergency.

The pink tam had a definite militant tilt, and her black high-heeled pumps struck the hard city pavement more in the manner of combat boots. Julie Chamber's was a "fighting walk," as her father so fondly called it.

And fight she would. Despite that old worn-out cliché about city hall.

It had finally come in the morning's mail: The long-dreaded official eviction notice, neatly typed on City of Chicago letterhead and signed by the mayor himself, in an almost illegible but nonetheless authoritative scrawl. Sitting behind her gray metal desk at the library, Julie had angrily torn the letter into pieces and tossed them into the wastebasket.

"I don't *believe* it! They're actually going to *do* it!"

For three years Julie had been both anticipating and dreading the formal edict from city hall, all the while praying that some timely miracle might thwart its arrival.

With the specter of impending destruction looming over one shoulder, Julie had hopefully been peeking over the other for the answer to her prayer. All she wanted was one of God Almighty's avenging angels— not a whole legion—just one capable, and perhaps a bit ferocious-looking, angel on special assignment, to spread his forbidding wings at the big double doors of the library and dare anyone to tear the old building down.

But Julie Chambers knew that God, in His infinite wisdom, sometimes said no to a prayer—be it the simple please of a small farm girl in Kansas or the well-phrased request of a city-dwelling journalism major.

Back on the farm, despite Julie's tearful entreaties to the Creator, one of his gentlest creatures, a tiny sick lamb, had died. And untimely rains had ruined an unharvested crop.

Here in the Windy City, the current subject of Julie's prayer was again a target of ruin: The century-old McDonough mansion destined to crumble to a pile of red-brick rubble at the hands of those helmeted demons of urban progress, the hired wrecking crew.

To Julie, it was more than merely a matter of destroying an old brick building. It was a strike against the city's very foundation, its rich architectural heritage.

But the most serious crime was against those who looked hopefully to the old mansion-turned-library as an oasis of culture in a desert of creeping blight—the Latinos and blacks who lived in the infamous midtown ghetto.

Now, with the opening of the morning's mail, it was official. The Midtown Branch Library would forever close its doors in June, and shortly after, its temporary head librarian was to begin boxing up its seven thousand books.

What the tersely phrased letter from the mayor did not—and need not—say was that the door-closing and book-packing would be accompanied by the unmistakable marching music of the relentlessly advancing wrecking crew.

The city's mild winter and freakishly warm and windless March had furthered the crew's advance. Already an ugly gaping swath had been bulldozed through condemned apartments and warehouses, each day drawing nearer the next intended victim—the McDonough mansion.

Tearing up the mayor's official notice had not

cooled Julie's anger; had, in fact, only fanned its flames.

"They can't *do* it!" she had insisted, pounding her fist on the metal desk.

Then, as she had sat rubbing her bruised hand, Julie's hot anger had slowly seethed into something more positive—burning determination.

Angel or no angel, she wouldn't *let* them do it!

With that, she had snatched up her hat and coat and stormed out of the library. And now, her four-block "fighting walk" ended at the glass door of the police station.

"I want a permit," she told the young red-haired officer behind the counter.

He had been busily writing, and now he glanced up at her with the bluest eyes she had ever seen.

"I've come for a permit," she told him again.

"Not for a gun, I hope."

There was concern in his husky voice, but Julie wasn't sure it was genuine—mostly because of a fleeting flicker of boyish mischief she thought she saw in those startlingly blue eyes.

"Of course not," she told him. "For a parade."

The policeman set down his ballpoint pen. "You're too late. St. Patrick's Day is already over."

"I don't mean *that* kind of a parade," she said with a quick toss of almost blue-black shoulder-length hair. "I mean people—and signs."

"People and signs," he echoed. "Could you possibly mean *picketing?* "

"Maybe."

"A good old-fashioned star-spangled protest?"

"Possibly." She was struggling not to show her mounting annoyance. "Definitely," she then told him. "A protest."

10

"Against what?"

"City Hall."

At that, the young officer slowly leaned back in his swivel chair and gave her an anything but in-the-line-of-duty appraisal. "Now what," he asked her, in deliberate, husky male syllables, "would a nice girl like you have against City Hall?"

"The fact," said Julie, "that they are going to tear down my library." She would later marvel at her own statement—that an old run-down two-story mansion in a strange city should have become "her library."

"Now that *is* serious," said the policeman. He sat forward in his chair, as if he thought the matter of tearing down anyone's library was, indeed, of great consequence. "What's the problem—dirty books?"

"Look!" she exploded. "I didn't come here to be insulted by some smart-aleck cop!"

She had never before used the word *cop* —in fact, she often scolded the children at the library for doing just that. Sometimes, of course, they used even worse words in referring to an officer of the law—blatant barnyard epithets picked up from the local street gangs.

If the officer behind the counter considered either *smart aleck* or *cop* in any way offensive, he didn't show it. Rather, he grinned slowly, parting his lips to reveal sturdy white teeth—one of them noticeably crooked.

"Gutsy, too. I like that."

"I'm not interested in what you like," Julie said through her own white, perfectly straight teeth, "only in getting a permit."

"And that," he said, rising and gathering up his scattered papers, "you'll have to get at City Hall."

An hour later, Julie Chambers slowly trudged down the steel steps of the elevated station, the fight long gone from her stride. The overworked axiom about fighting City Hall didn't seem trite anymore. She briefly thought of once again trying to see the local alderman. But, recalling last month's abortive attempt, she quickly brushed that thought aside.

Alighting from the shuttle bus somewhat later, she was still so steeped in frustration that she was not aware of being followed. When her pursuer caught up with her at the pawn shop—still a good distance from the library—and lightly touched her arm, Julie gave a small startled gasp.

"Hi."

Her first impulse was to ignore him. But she found that impossible, considering his uniform, his red hair, and that one crooked tooth.

"How'd you make out?" he asked.

"Well—" She acknowledged his presence without breaking her stride. "I didn't bother trying to see the mayor again."

"Smart move."

"Or his snooty secretary."

"Smart again."

"I did see someone in permits, though."

"And?"

"He said a parade was definitely out. For that I'd need an organization."

"I could've told you that."

"And as for picketing—or protesting—I'd probably end up needing a good lawyer."

"Could've told you that, too."

She stopped dead in her tracks. "Why *didn't* you?"

"Because I'm a smart aleck," he grinned. "Remember?"

The officer took her by the arm then, and began steering her toward an unmarked car parked at the curb. Of dubious vintage, and badly in need of a paint job, it was what the neighborhood children would irreverently dub an "old beater."

"Where to?" he asked, opening the car door. "I'm off duty now."

"Really, I'm quite able—"

"Oh, come on." He urged her onto the front seat of his car. "I never molest girls when I'm in uniform."

In total contrast to his flippant manner at the station, he now seemed to show genuine interest in Julie's problem. As they inched back to the library through the lunch-hour traffic, she told him that the city, to install an on-ramp for the new intracity expressway, was going to demolish the Midtown Branch Library.

"That so?" he remarked, as if such information was fresh news. Later, Julie would wonder if it really was. Even the most duty-bound cop must find time to read the newspaper.

But having finally found a willing ear, Julie went on with her longtime complaint against the city, ending with the fact that she was Midtown's head librarian— something at which she continued to marvel.

Keeping his blue eyes fixed on the traffic, her driver nodded sympathetically. "I guess the want ads aren't exactly loaded with jobs for librarians."

"It's not my job that matters," she told him, "it's the library. The fact that it won't *be* there anymore."

"I'm sure they'll find another spot for it."

"That's just the point—they *can't*.There isn't a vacant lot in the whole ward—except Steiner's *Sommergarten.* "

"Please—not *that!* " He slapped his right hand to his heart. "Where would I spend my Saturday nights?"

His exaggerated response irritated her. *Her* statement had not been an exaggeration. Besides the children's playground and the lawn surrounding the old McDonough mansion, the only other piece of open land in the bleak brick-and-brownstone ghetto was the outdoor garden at the Blue Angel, a one-story German restaurant sandwiched between two decrepit, soot-blackened tenements.

Julie had heard via neighborhood lore that its starstruck owner, Herman Steiner, had named it after a somewhat seamy German inn in an old Marlene Dietrich movie.

Though she had never been inside Steiner's Blue Angel, she doubted it was in any way shady—except for the two giant oak trees in the outdoor garden attached to it.

Walking the six blocks to her bus each night, Julie passed the Blue Angel. Though there never seemed to be any shortage of cars parked at the curb, the adjacent garden sat empty in the winter. But, in the summer, the murmur of voices and clink of tableware and the scent of char-broiled steaks, bratwurst and sauerkraut drifted from behind the thick privet hedge.

Not once had she considered the fact that Steiner's lantern-lit *Sommergarten*—at least three lots wide—was the only other open piece of land in the entire

14

ward. Her mentioning it now as a possible site for the Midtown Branch Library showed how desperate she was.

"What about an empty storefront?" Her driver broke into her thoughts. "There's no shortage of those."

Julie shook her head. "There's not a store building large enough. Besides, that's how the branch first started. We have over seven thousand books now," she added, not without a tinge of pride.

"You don't say."

Was he truly impressed or was he making fun of her?

"Not only that—" she went on, "It's the building itself. Over a hundred years old."

"Yeah," he nodded. "I know the old dump."

"It's not an old dump, it's a—"

"Firetrap."

Julie tightly pressed her lips together, deciding to end the conversation right there. He was as bad as all the others—the city fathers included—who couldn't care less that an old neglected mansion might actually be a priceless historical landmark.

If it wasn't functional, it deserved to be blown up. If it was in the way of an expressway, it needed to be bulldozed. It didn't seem to matter that the old McDonough mansion had been built by one of the city's first families. The fact that some three thousand inner-city residents would be without a local library didn't carry much weight, either.

But, though Julie had decided to drop the subject, her uniformed chauffeur persisted. "And just what do you hope to accomplish by a protest?"

"Change their minds."

"About the expressway? Forget it."

"No. I simply want them to move the on-ramp over about five hundred feet."

He thought for a moment. "And just what is there—over about five hundred feet?"

"You're a policeman! You ought to know. The rest of the old McDonough estate—the city playground."

"Oh, yeah," he eventually nodded.

Until the city had erected a barbed-wire topped chain-link fence with a foolproof lock on its gate, the children's playground had been a nighttime arena for settling the differences between the two always-feuding midtown ghetto street gangs. More than once someone had called the police.

Moments later the off-duty policeman parked his car in the no-parking zone next to that very playground. When he tossed his cap onto the back seat and loosened his tie before turning to her, Julie had the feeling she had not been picked up by the average police officer.

Nor was he a run-of-the-mill redhead. The color of his thick regulation-cropped hair was more a burnt sienna than an actual red, and his generous expressive brows over his thick-lashed eyes, were a deep brown. And those incredibly blue eyes—never had she seen such a disarming blend of sensuality and boyish mischief.

Julie observed all this in one brief yet thorough feminine glance which included the officer's undeniably male, yet vulnerable, mouth—the way his upper lip puckered ever so slightly over the one crooked tooth. She didn't fail to notice, too, the fact that his left hand, on the steering wheel, was ringless.

"Shame on you," he said, sliding his arm across the back of the seat.

Julie felt a sudden rush of blood to her cheeks, certain he was chiding her for her own less-than-professional appraisal of him.

But now he was nodding to the window, obviously referring to the sandy area within the chain-link fence. "You should be ashamed, trying to rip off the poor little kids' playground."

It was only then that Julie became aware of the laughter and shouts of children mingled with the noontime noises of the busy city. And when she turned her own face to the window, she saw several youngsters romping in the playground. Still battling her sudden warm flush, it occurred to her that this time last year those same children had been huddled in their own private rat-infested firetraps, trying to keep warm during one of the city's worst freezes.

"There's more than one form of exercise, you know," she told her driver, now even closer to her on the seat. "Do you know some of those children can't even read—or speak English, for that matter?"

"Then why do they need—"

"A library? As a place where they can *learn* to read and speak the language! That's part of my—our—daily children's program."

"How about that."

Julie didn't bother telling him about her other programs for the parents of those underprivileged children—English, child-care, first-aid and cooking classes.

A cop who thought the library was an "old dump" probably couldn't care less about what went on under its ancient roof—so long as it was all legal and didn't

17

disturb anyone's peace ... and didn't sometime prove he was right about the mansion's being a "firetrap."

Now he was leaning toward the window, as it to get a better look at what lay just beyond the playground—the old mansion for which this gutsy female crusader would move an expressway on-ramp.

"That's asking an awful lot," he said with his cheek just inches from hers, " ... redesigning a roadway when more than half's already cut through."

"I'm sure," she said, opening her door, "that all those brainy city engineers could think of *something*."

Walking down the sidewalk to the old converted McDonough Mansion with her personal police escort, Julie noted he was at least a half-foot taller than she, maybe five-nine or ten, but certainly not tall by today's standards for men.

His boyish profile made it hard to guess his age, but she was sure he was not a wet-behind-the-ears rookie. His easy chin-high, almost arrogant gait spoke of his assurance, both with his sex and with his station in life. Every step of the way, Julie was acutely aware that her escort—every compact, uniformed inch of him—was a man.

"So what do you plan to do?" he asked her just before they reached the wrought-iron gate.

"About what?"

"About the library."

"Oh." She had forgotten momentarily just how and why they had met. "What I should've done three years ago. Protest."

"How?"

"Like the man said. Good old-fashioned star-spangled sitdown."

She had expected him to grin at hearing his own slightly edited punchline. But he was deadly serious.

"When?"

"Soon as I can muster my troops."

"Where?"

"Where else?" She nodded over her shoulder, toward the lake.

"City Hall? You *will* need a lawyer."

Julie let out her second little gasp of the day when she suddenly saw a crowd of people—some sitting, others standing—on the library steps, outside the double doors that should have been opened over an hour ago.

"Looks like you've got a little sitdown going already," he quipped, as they walked through the wrought-iron gate.

"Good grief—I *forgot!*"

After fishing in her bag for the library key, inwardly chiding herself for such thoughtlessness, Julie caught fearful looks on the black or tan faces of her Monday morning patrons. Had their favorite librarian been arrested?

"It's all right," Julie told them in her stilted high school Spanish. *"El policia es mi amigo."* The policeman is my friend.

Later, she would wonder at her statement. Calling "friend" someone who had mocked her, contradicted her and sent her on a wild goose chase.

If the policeman thought this was strange, he gave no sign. Rather, he gave her a casual salute before leaving her at the gate. "See you around, *mi amiga.*"

From the big curtainless bay window in the main reading room, Julie watched as the policeman strode

19

down the sidewalk to the playground, got into his old car, and drove away.

"Trouble?" asked Sarah Brown, a stout black lady who was also watching from the window.

"No, I don't think so," Julie answered. "At least I hope not."

But the rest of that day the Midtown Branch librarian had a good deal of trouble keeping her mind on her work. And that night, abed in her roomy lakeshore apartment, Julie was still thinking about the red-haired, ringless, crooked-toothed policeman.

And she didn't even know his name.

CHAPTER 2

JULIE SOON LEARNED the name of a certain red-haired Chicago cop when she appeared with the "arresting officer"—before one of the judges of the Cook County Circuit Court.

On her way to the courthouse in the back seat of a cab, Julie was certain the East Coast papers had gotten the story through the wire service. What must her parents be thinking? Yet, there was a chance, especially if her father's one-man boycott of the daily newspapers was still in force, that her parents might not know of her arrest.

Julie wasn't quite sure what she herself should make of it all. She still was somewhat amazed to find herself caught up in such a futile one-woman crusade against City Hall.

When she had landed at O'Hare three years ago— the ink on her college diploma barely dry—working in a library was something that had never crossed her mind. Actually, the list of possible big city employers had been short—newspaper, television studio, advertising agency. It hadn't mattered which, as long as she could apply the natural gifts God had given her—a talent for turning a clever phrase and the sheer love of the English language. At least those gifts wouldn't lie fallow on a farm.

But she had soon learned that the Michigan Avenue media wizards had not been holding their breath in anticipation of Julie Chamber's dropping out of Kansas. And the starry-eyed farm girl's yellow-brick road to a dream career had become three inches of yellow telephone pages and the classified ad section of the *Chicago Tribune*.

Because rainbow-chasing writers had to eat and pay rent like everyone else, Julie had—only as a stopgap survival measure—applied for the advertised job of library aide at the Midtown Branch Library. And, she had argued with herself, working in a library really wouldn't be that far afield. She would still be handling her favorite tools, though they were written and edited by someone else. Besides, in the quiet of a library—with its usual snail's pace routine—she might even find the time to write her *own* book.

Such had been Julie's wound-licking thoughts the morning of her interview with the Midtown head librarian.

From its address, in the most congested part of the city, she had expected the branch library to be one of those cramped, converted storefronts with more window glass than floor space—its scant shelves stocked with only a token supply of books for those readers too far from the big main library on the lakefront.

Instead, Julie had been pleasantly surprised to find the printed address in the classified ad also sharply chiseled into one of the gray stone stanchions of an imposing wrought-iron fence that surrounded—along with a wide expanse of trim green grass—a charming old red-brick mansion. Replete with hand-carved wooden fretwork and stained-glass windows, and boasting two pointed turrets and three chimneys, the house brought to mind those brooding mysterious Victorian mansions in the plot of every Gothic novel—and Julie had read more than her share of those back in high school.

Behind the huge oaken double doors, Julie found a small foyer—now obviously a coatroom—studded with wall hooks randomly decorated with jackets, sweaters and shawls, evidence to the fact that Chicago's spring weather was as fickle as a school girl, changing without notice.

Beyond the anteroom lay what had no doubt once been a spacious and elegant parlor, now the main reading room of the Midtown Branch Library—its fading papered walls lined with book-laden shelves; its bare oak floor burdened with long, anything-but-elegant reading tables; its ornately wood-manteled fireplace, the backdrop for the clumsy checkout desk.

Completely taken aback by the number of books, Julie was no less surprised at the number of people browsing at the shelves or already reading at the tables, and at the seemingly endless parade of children up and down the open banistered staircase, to and from what she would later learn was the Children's Reading Room.

But the building's charm and its hivelike reader activity were a misleading prelude to her encounter with the Midtown head librarian.

23

The interview took place in a small closetlike room at the rear of the house which Julie supposed had once been the butler's pantry. The room barely accommodated the librarian's gun-metal gray desk, matching gray filing cabinet, and an almost ceiling-high shelf of newspapers, pamphlets, and catalogs which Julie assumed were the necessary working tools of any librarian.

The head librarian, a slender, attractive brownish-haired woman perhaps in her midthirties, was at first crisp and courteous. But Ellen Gray briefly scanned Julie's carefully typed resumé, seemingly as unimpressed as the Michigan Avenue media moguls. The fact that Julie Chambers had graduated in the top 10 percent of her class at Kansas State with numerous creative writing awards and, in her senior year, had been editor of her high school newspaper failed to impress her potential employer.

Julie was unaware of how long the aide position had been advertised in the newspapers, and she had no way of knowing then that she was the one-and-only applicant—or why.

"How soon can you start?" asked Ellen Gray, casually handing the resumé back to Julie across her cluttered desk.

"Right away," said Julie, her eyes wide. Without further ado she was being given the job. "Tomorrow, if you like."

"Good."

If the answer conveyed any feeling at all, it was that the Midtown librarian had just completed one more of a thousand tedious tasks that were part of a long, wearisome day—far from being over.

And Julie did not miss the woman's wry mouth-

24

twist of annoyance as another troop of children thundered down the wooden stairs, directly overhead, nor the unsuccessfully muffled comment—something that sounded to Julie like "ignorant brats."

The librarian once again turned her attention to her newly hired assistant who was still standing, simply because there wasn't room for another chair in the converted pantry.

"Of course you know the job is just temporary."

"Well, yes . . . " Julie answered, though she thought the "temporary" aspect existed only in her own mind, a way to tread water until she became a swimming success behind a typewriter in one of the carpeted suites of either the Sears Tower or the Hancock Building.

Despite all the previous turndowns, she was determined not to give up her goal of infiltrating the world of mass media—mainly, because she considered it her personal, God-given mission as a Christian.

Like her father, Julie had become increasingly dismayed at the materialistic—even pagan—aura of television commercials and programs. The weekday soap operas, with their flaunting of pre- and extramarital sex, were especially distressing.

Even more disturbing than the deluge of sex and violence on the tube was the relentlessly pounded-home gospel according to TV, preached daily to the "Me Generation." It had very strict self-styled commandments: Thou shalt not deny thyself anything that feels good, looks good, or tastes good; and while so indulging thyself, thou shalt also not wear any size larger than ten; thou shalt never be guilty of body odor, bad breath, or dandruff; and thou shalt never be guilty of that deadliest of sins—growing (or even looking) old.

25

Being forever young—feeling, looking and smelling good—seemed to be all there was to life. Another—*eternal* life? Well, to accept that, you would have to believe in God. And "Jesus of Nazareth" would have to mean more than the title of a popular film dug out of the archives and rerun at the appropriate season to boost Nielsen ratings.

Such a godless, one-life-to-live philosophy was not surprising to Julie, considering its source. While doing research for her final college term paper, she had stumbled upon the results of a survey of journalists—both in print and on TV. Eighty-six percent admitted to never or seldom attending church services; nine out of ten were proabortion; eighty-five percent believed premarital sex was not immoral, and more than half believed there was nothing wrong with adultery. Among TV writers, producers, and executives—those responsible for the nation's "prime-time" shows—the percentages were even higher.

Back on the farm, Julie's father had long ago stopped watching television. When their small black-and-white set went on the blink, he never bothered to get it repaired or buy a new one. Eventually he had stopped reading the newspapers, too, reaching for his Bible for both solace and security in a world which he considered totally in the clutches of the devil.

For Thou wilt light my candle: The Lord my God will enlighten my darkness.

While Julie felt much the same as her father—perhaps disagreeing as to the scope of Satan's grasp—she did not think the answer was pulling either the Psalms or the Gospels over one's head like a scriptural security blanket. Rather than put on

26

biblical blinders, she felt compelled to search for a way to cope with, then perhaps combat, the godless daily dogma on the airwaves and in print.

Some of her seeking had led her to proverbs other than those in the Good Book, and one particularly pithy bit of Chinese wisdom had found a welcome niche in her writer's brain: "It is better to light one candle than to curse the darkness."

And hadn't our Lord Himself warned against hiding one's light under a basket? In one of His many poignant parables, hadn't Jesus also cautioned against burying one's talents?

Thus, even before graduation from college, Julie Chambers had vowed to use her God-given talent in becoming a "light"—albeit feeble—in the dark world of mass media.

And if her determination had sometimes wavered, it was finally solidified by another prophetic pronouncement—also discovered while doing research—by the noted American statesman, Daniel Webster, well over a century ago:

If religious books are not widely circulated among the masses in this country, I do not know what is going to become of us as a nation. If truth be not diffused, error will be; if God and His Word are not known and received, the devil and his works will gain the ascendancy; if the evangelical volume does not reach every hamlet, the pages of a corrupt and licentious literature will; if the power of the Gospel is not felt throughout the length and breadth of the land, anarchy and misrule, degradation and misery, corruption and darkness, will reign without mitigation or end.

Julie had been both chilled and challenged by Webster's ominous prophecy, spoken back in 1823, which surely seemed to be having its frightening fulfillment today. She had thus charted a course which would take her headlong into those dark waters her father so religiously tried to avoid.

Her target was Chicago, her strategy nothing less than infiltrating the ranks of the very propaganda machine she considered so delinquent. No matter that the machine already had rejected the small cog from Kansas; she would not stop trying to be an integral— perhaps reforming—part.

And if the job at the Midtown Branch Library was only temporary, that was all the better. Still, she couldn't help wondering why, and before the end of her brief morning interview with Ellen Gray, Julie asked the disgruntled head librarian just that.

"Don't you read the newspapers?" was the sharp reply.

Julie felt a rush of color to her cheeks. "Not lately. At least not the headlines."

As a student of journalism, a writer, it hurt to make such an admission. But Julie had neglected the front pages of the *Chicago Tribune* for what, at the moment, had interested her more—the help wanted ads in the back pages.

"Well, if you *had* read them," the woman said, straightening a small pile of papers on her desk, "you'd know the building eventually is going to be demolished."

"*Demolished!* A beautiful old place like this?"

Julie's sinking feeling was the same as when she thought of her grandmother's lovely old octagonal house back in Kansas. It had, along with a number of other old homes, been bulldozed to make way for a shopping center.

The Midtown librarian glanced about in a sweeping arc as if to encompass the entire building still known as the old McDonough Mansion. Her expression implied that it wouldn't bother her one bit if the wrecking crew arrived that very moment.

"The city needs the land for the new expressway," she said, rising behind her steel desk. "In fact, the westbound on-ramp should come through just about here." And she nodded, with yet another mouth-twist of malevolent satisfaction, toward the children's stairway overhead.

"That help-wanted ad," said the woman, "was a bit misleading, I'm afraid."

You can say that again, Julie thought wryly.

"But of course, you can say just so much in so many words."

Julie wondered what other pertinent information had been left out of the five-line classified ad.

"You *will* be assisting me, of course," said Ellen Gray, "but only for two weeks."

Julie's dark eyebrows went up. "I'll say that's *temporary.*"

"Oh, don't worry—you'll still have a job." The woman gave a little ironic smile. "Maybe more of a job than you bargained for."

This last remark left Julie feeling somewhat confused, and a bit uneasy. "What do you mean?"

"Well, let's put it this way, honey." Ellen Gray spread her palms on the desk and leaned forward, almost companionably. "I have been rotting in this rat-trap, just waiting for you to show up. I'll give you two weeks of my time—to show you the ropes—and then, my dear, I am going to split."

29

The last word—seemingly out of character for any librarian—caught Julie off guard and she had some trouble suppressing a small laugh.

"I am leaving this God-forsaken ghetto and going on to greener pastures," said Ellen Gray with obvious relief punctuating each syllable.

"But if you're leaving," said Julie, "who's going to *run* the place?"

"I'll give you three guesses."

Julie needed only one. "But, I don't know the first thing about running a library!"

"This isn't a library, honey, it's a circus. You think those people out there can actually *read* any of those books?"

Julie followed the woman's nod, glancing over her shoulder into the adjacent reference room—originally the dining room of the old mansion. Passing through it on her way to the pantry, she had been aware that it, too, was crowded with readers. Only now did she see that all of them were Hispanics or blacks.

"Your biggest job," Ellen Gray assured her, "will be keeping enough tissue in the johns. And," she added with a meaningful nod toward the children's stairway, "breaking up fights."

"Eventually," the librarian went on, "you'll get the closing order from City Hall. And then you'll have the neat little job of packing up the books—all seven thousand of them."

Julie tried to visualize cartons and cartons of books to be boxed and delivered to—she didn't bother asking where.

But she did ask, "How soon is *eventually?*"

The woman shrugged. "Who knows?" She might as well have said, "Who cares?" It was obvious *she* didn't. "You still want the job?"

30

This time it was Julie who shrugged. "I guess so— but only until something better comes along."

"So be it," said Ellen Gray.

And in Julie's mind the woman was washing her hands, as if she now considered herself off the hook by having finally recruited her own replacement, regardless of how temporary.

There was an awkward pause then, and the writer in Julie felt compelled to fill it.

"Where will you be going?" she asked Ellen Gray, trying to sound genuinely interested. Actually, she had begun to dislike her temporary boss.

"I have a new position waiting for me out in the suburbs."

"That's nice."

"As children's librarian."

This time Julie's laugh spilled out before she could stop it. How ridiculous! A person who so obviously disliked children couldn't *want* such a job. Only then did it occur to Julie that Ellen Gray's problem with these particular children might not be their age or their boundless energy; rather, their color.

The Midtown librarian drew back as if Julie's impulsive laugh had been a slap in the face. She stood upright and coldly stared at her newly hired assistant. "Where I'm going, the children will be *civilized*."

"You mean *white*, don't you?"

If the woman's earlier stare had been cold, now it was solid ice. "What are you, some kind of civil rights nut?"

"I'm a Christian," Julie said simply.

"Then just watch whom you're accusing of prejudice. Or maybe you don't bother to read your Bible, either."

31

"I *do* read the Bible." In fact, Julie had the Good Book—or at least part of it—in her handbag that very moment. A small pocket-sized New Testament, handy for reading on the bus, or sitting hours on end in personnel offices, was with her at all times.

"Then judge not that ye not be judged."

It was a direct reprimand from the Book in question, and now it was Julie's turn to wince. And didn't she deserve it? Hadn't her mother often cautioned her against self-righteousness?

"I'm sorry," Julie said softly. "I truly am."

"Forget it," said Ellen Gray. "Besides, you're probably right." She sat back down behind her steel desk as if suddenly she were very tired. She nodded once more toward the crowded reference room. "And who knows? Maybe you can help those poor souls."

"Oh, I seriously doubt that."

Julie was sure her Creator had bigger and better plans for Julie Chambers. Besides, what could anyone possibly do to help any "poor souls" in so short a time?

Though she would not have believed it the day of the interview, Julie and Ellen Gray actually parted friends, promising to keep in touch.

Nor did Julie have any idea then that her temporary job at the library would end up stretching over weeks, then months, into what was now over three years.

In that time, Julie had slowly learned what she *could* do—a good deal more than merely keeping tissue in the johns and refereeing fights. As each new need or opportunity arose, another program was added to the library's calendar of activities.

Somewhere along the line, the Midtown Branch

Library had become *her* library and its patrons *her* people. And each day Julie Chambers's campus-born dream of a Michigan Avenue media career was pushed farther and farther into the background.

"This is why you went to college?" her father asked in one of her early phone calls home. "To play denmother to a bunch of kids?"

"God works in mysterious ways," she had answered, certain her God-fearing father would not quarrel with that. Now she wondered if she hadn't really stayed at the library because it was easier than going back out on Michigan Avenue for some more bruises to her battered ego. To imply that the Lord may have led her to the Midtown Library because of some mysterious divine plan could be self-serving, couldn't it?

"Besides," she told her father, "I'm also writing a book."

Peter Chambers' answer to that was familiar. She might as well have stayed home on the farm if all she was going to do was write a book.

It seemed that her father would never stop hoping his only daughter would return to Kansas and marry some "local yokel" who would dutifully take over the family farm. Julie prayed her father would never know the truth—how much she hated the farm, how she'd rather die than go back to a life of gathering eggs, slopping pigs, milking cows and pickling cucumbers. Even in college she had not been able to escape the daily farm routine, having been a commuter rather than a resident student.

When she had boarded the plane for Chicago three years ago, Julie had been determined that—whatever else might happen—she would never go back to the farm. Gone forever were the days of the hayseed-in-her-hair farmer's daughter.

Only after his mild heart attack two years earlier did Peter Chambers stop needling his daughter to come back home. Indeed, he sold the family farm and bought a Florida condominium, where he and Julie's mother were now enjoying the much-advertised joys of retirement living.

"When are you coming down for a visit?" was her father's question when she called her parents every weekend.

"Just as soon as they close the place," had been her usual reply.

But that had been before she had started all her library programs and gotten so involved with her people; before she had become angry about the city's new expressway and its hired wrecking crew; before she had become so obsessed with fighting the senseless destruction of the old McDonough Mansion.

It had also been before all her polite letters—to Chicago's mayor and to the editor of the *Chicago Tribune* — and before her futile attempts to see both the mayor and the local alderman.

Last week it had finally come in the mail—the much-dreaded official eviction notice from City Hall. And Julie had known it was going to take an out-and-out protest to save the building and all that went on under its century-old roof.

The immediate result had been two encounters with a certain Chicago policeman. Today would make three. For, at the end of her cab ride, she would face the cocky red-haired officer again in court.

And whatever else might come of it, Julie was sure of one thing—she'd finally know his name.

CHAPTER 3

"PATROLMAN TERRANCE J. BRANNIGAN," the officer answered the judge.

Julie had never been to court before, but she knew this little trial was nothing like the ones in Perry Mason movies. It wasn't even being held in a courtroom, but in a small wood-paneled office which she suspected was the judge's chamber.

The judge, dressed in an ordinary business suit, was seated behind his desk, his back to a large bold-framed portrait of Abraham Lincoln.

In addition to a fast-fingered court reporter, the only other people in the room—also seated on leather-upholstered chairs—were Julie herself and the uniformed officer who had just now, for the record, identified himself.

"And you are the arresting officer?" was the judge's second question.

"Yes, sir."

"On what charges?"

35

Patrolman Brannigan shifted on his seat and focused his blue eyes directly on Julie. Julie focused hers on Lincoln's beard.

"Disturbing the peace, blocking the entrance to a public building and parading without a permit," said Brannigan.

The weary-looking judge adjusted his glasses and studied the dossier before him on his desk. Julie's was the last case on the docket.

"Miss Julie Chambers," the judge now addressed her, "it says here that you are a librarian. Is that true?"

"Yes," she respectfully answered. "And no."

The judge's shaggy eyebrows shot up. "Yes and no? How can it be both?"

"Well, you see—I *am* a librarian, but I never planned to be. I didn't study to be one."

"But you *do* work at the Midtown Branch Library."

"Yes, sir."

"And just what do you do at the library?"

"Well, I—" What was the judge getting at? "I—sort of do everything."

"You mean you run the library?"

"I have to. There's nobody else there. *Working* there, I mean."

"Then we are correct in saying you are the head librarian?"

"Well," she reluctantly conceded, "I guess so."

"Yes or no?"

"Yes."

The judge sighed, much like a dentist who had finally succeeded in extracting a stubborn tooth. "And as a presumably literate librarian"— with his pencil he tapped the dossier before him—"you didn't know that such things are against the law?"

Julie's heart suddenly began to pound. "What things?" she asked feebly.

"*What things?*" the judge echoed her incredulously. "The things this officer has just charged you with—disturbing the peace, blocking the entrance to a public building and parading without a permit. You didn't know such things are against the law?"

"No, sir. I mean . . . yes, sir."

"Well, which is it? Yes or no?"

"Yes, sir. I knew they were against the law."

At the time, Julie had justified her actions by recalling that even Jesus had become angry, overturning the tables of the money-changers at the temple. She had, however—perhaps conveniently—forgotten that the humble Carpenter's Son also had carefully obeyed Roman law—no matter how unjust or oppressive.

The judge looked down again at his papers and then over to the arresting officer. "It says here—a crowd. Just how many would you estimate?"

"About fifty," said Brannigan.

"Twenty," Julie corrected him.

The judge made a little penciled note. "Twenty what?"

"Concerned, civic-minded citizens," said Julie.

"Kids," said Brannigan.

On the day in question, Julie had waited until the children came into the library for the afternoon story hour. She originally had planned on recruiting all of them, but had ended up choosing only the children who ordinarily stayed late at the library because their mothers worked.

Her chosen few had been delighted with the prospect of "being in a parade," as Julie had put it, and they had been happy to let her herd them, like little sheep, downtown on the elevated train. They had thought it great fun to march up and down in front of City Hall with little American flags and Julie's handmade signs: SAVE OUR LIBRARY! None of them had expected, or much less understood, the grand finale: their parade mistress's arrest.

The robeless judge made another note with his pencil and then wearily took off his glasses. "And you—" he said, focusing his tired eyes on Julie, "a civil servant of the public, fully cognizant of the fact that you were breaking the law, willfully induced innocent children to do the same?"

"Well, I wouldn't put it exactly like that."

"Yes or no."

Julie lowered her eyes. "Yes."

The judge set down his glasses and loudly sighed. "One hundred dollars or ten days."

"One hundred dollars!" Julie clutched her handbag. "I don't *have* a hundred dollars!"

He punctuated his ruling with a tap of his pencil. "Ten days."

And with that, both the judge and the arresting officer got up and left the chamber.

Julie sat frozen on the leather-upholstered seat.

Ten days? Ten days of *what?* Surely the judge hadn't meant ten days in *jail!* He *couldn't* have meant locking her up in the county jail with all those common *criminals!* But what then? He certainly couldn't have meant a free ten-day vacation at the Chicago Hilton!

Ten days in jail!

As she was staring in shock at the picture of "Honest Abe" behind the judge's empty desk, Julie's imagination suddenly took over. *Her long hair was cut to just above the ears and she was wearing a prison uniform. In the cell with her were three other women—all black-rooted blondes with heavily made-up faces.*

"What you in for, sister?" asked the most painted of the three.

"Parading," said Julie.

"Hah! That's a new name for it!" laughed the second woman.

"Where?" asked the third.

"City Hall."

"Hey—" said the first woman. "That's my territory!"

"Oh, no!" said Julie. "You don't understand!"

"Oh, don't we?"

"I'm not a—" She couldn't even say the word. "I'm a librarian."

"Oh, sure," said the second woman. "and I'm a captain in the Salvation Army."

"What'd they give you?" asked the third woman.

"Ten days."

"Well, enjoy 'em," said the first woman. "Because when you get out, I'm going to give you this!" And she made a sharp throat-cutting finger swipe at Julie's neck.

It was at that precise point in her frightful fantasy that Julie felt a large hand on her shoulder.

"Oh!"

Looking up at one of the black-suited courthouse bailiffs, her imagined prison-cell nightmare became even more real. The man surely had come to slap the cuffs on her and haul her into the waiting paddy wagon.

"You can go now," said the bailiff.

"Go?" she said dully. "Where?"

"Home—or wherever."

Julie continued to stare up at the man, sure she had misunderstood.

"One for the books," he said, shaking his head. "First he arrests you and then he bails you out."

It took some time for Julie to digest that. And still she wasn't sure she understood. "*He* paid my fine— *Brannigan?*"

"That's right," the man nodded. "You're free as a butterfly."

Butterfly?

Julie tried to smile at the man's analogy, but at the moment she felt more like a grounded moth. Still shrouded in all her nightmarish thoughts about paddy wagons and prison mates, she slowly got up from her seat.

Clutching her handbag, she turned to the open door of the judge's chamber to see her fine-paying benefactor waiting for her in the hall. Mustering her few remaining fragments of pride, Julie lifted her chin and walked out of the room, passing the red-haired patrolman as if he were merely another picture hanging on the courthouse wall.

But the officer was right on her heels: down the hall, through the foyer and down the courthouse steps. He finally caught her arm out on the sidewalk.

"Is that any way to say thank you?"

"For what—almost throwing me in the clink?" She fiercely pulled her arm free.

"Any other policeman would have done the same," he said, falling in step beside her. "You're lucky it *wasn't* some other cop."

"If you mean the hundred dollars—you'll get it back on payday."

"Another cop would also have charged you with abusive language."

"Oh, now really!" She stopped just short of the crosswalk. "I hardly think the word *stinker*—"

"Unladylike, then,"

As he had done the first day they met, Brannigan took her by the arm again and steered her toward his old car, parked at the curb.

"You don't expect me to—"

"You'll never get a cab at *this* hour."

Once again Julie pulled her arm free. "I wouldn't get into that old beater with you, if it was the last bus out of *Berlin!*"

She was about to do just that—get on a bus—when she got the next offer of a ride. And this one she didn't refuse. Out of the corner of her eye, Julie saw the dark-haired, dark-suited young man briskly striding toward her.

"Hello, there. Remember me?"

She was about to shake her head no when she vaguely recalled having seen him somewhere.

"Bill Whittaker," he said. "At the alderman's office."

"Oh, yes."

Bill Whittaker had been behind the front desk when she had gone in, over a month ago, to see Alderman Paddy Fowler. Whittaker had given her a polite, but efficient brushoff.

41

"I tried to get to the bench before your case came up," he now told her, "but I got tied up in traffic."

"Really?" She gave him a doubtful look, not quite sure why anyone—especially the alderman's bouncer—would want to witness her little courtroom comeuppance.

"Mister Fowler is quite interested in your case."

"Well, I'm afraid he's a bit late. The fine's already been paid."

"I know," he said ruefully. "Someone beat me to it."

Glancing in the direction Brannigan's car had taken, Julie felt a tiny twinge of remorse at having so rudely brushed off her red-haired liberator. After all, he had only been doing his duty when he arrested her—and he certainly had not been obligated to pay her fine. At the same time, she wondered why Alderman Paddy Fowler would want to pay it.

"As I said," Bill Whittaker continued, as if he were answering her unspoken question, "Mister Fowler is quite interested in your cause."

Silently, Julie marveled that her case had now become a cause.

"You mean the library, of course."

"Exactly," said Whittaker. "He wondered if you might not come in now to see him."

Paddy Fowler had not had the time to see Julie Chambers five weeks ago. Suddenly the situation was reversed. Why? But her wonder was quickly buried under the hope that finally, finally someone with some clout was willing to listen to her.

"I'm parked about four blocks away," said Whittaker apologetically.

"No problem," said Julie. She was going to add

"for a butterfly," but considering Whittaker's serious, businesslike manner, she decided against it. If she were to make the right impression on Alderman Paddy Fowler, she certainly did not want to start out by acting frivolous with his aide.

Had she been inclined to rate a man by the kind of car he drove, Bill Whittaker would have scored a ten. His car was nothing less than a sleek, black Cadillac. Even the keys looked expensive, as did his dark three-piece designer suit and the trim leather attaché case between them on the front seat.

Julie figured him to be in his late twenties, yet with the blasé air of a much older man—as if life no longer held any surprises for him. He was exceptionally good looking and, in the well-tailored suit, could easily have posed for one of those slick Brooks Brothers ads in some magazine.

But his Cadillac pulled no special weight in the rush-hour traffic. By the time they reached the alderman's office, the street lights were on and Julie's stomach was talking about dinner.

Alderman Paddy Fowler—a redfaced, cigar-chewing ward boss—was just like his pictures. He also gave Julie the impression of a red-carpet reception as he ushered her into his inner sanctum—a small room at the back of a gold-and-black lettered storefront. Fowler lowered his stocky frame into the chair behind his cluttered desk and offered Julie the seat opposite him. Bill Whittaker leaned against a wall with his arms folded. After glancing in his direction, Julie quickly uncrossed her legs and straightened her skirt.

"I'm sorry I wasn't in the last time you were here," said Fowler.

"I'm sure you're a very busy man," said Julie, recalling the reek of fresh cigar smoke the day she had stopped in.

The alderman shuffled some papers around on his desk. "What's all this jazz about the old library?"

"I thought surely you must have read about it in the papers," said Julie.

"I learned a long time ago to ignore ninety percent of what I read in the papers," said Fowler. "Especially when they quote me," he added under his breath. "I'd rather get it straight from the horse's mouth."

Had she not been so intent on making a good impression, the farmer's daughter might have given the alderman her own observation's about horses' mouths. As it was, she merely shifted her handbag on her lap, took a deep breath and began.

"Well . . . " The whole story of the Midtown Branch Library poured forth—the past three years' reincarnation as a thriving community center; the tragic mistake it would be for the city to tear down such a lovely old landmark; all those letters; two attempts to see the mayor; her sidewalk protest, which had gotten her arrested.

When she ended her story, Fowler lay his cigar in the ashtray. "I like that—a girl with guts."

"It must be contagious."

Fowler gave her an odd look, not knowing, of course, that she was referring to a certain red-haired citizen who also claimed to like gutsy girls. Such an affinity, though, had not prevented her arrest and she could only wonder now where any alliance with this cigar-chewing councilman might lead. But what else could he have in mind other than allowing her to plead her cause before his fellow members of the city council?

"Just how old *are* you?" asked Fowler.

"Twenty-five last month," she told him, though she couldn't see what difference her age made.

"Married?"

"No."

"Why not?"

The question's bluntness left her with her mouth hanging open. It was the same question, more subtly phrased, that she had recently been hearing from her parents.

"I'd think some guy'd have grounded a cute little chick like you a long time ago," said Fowler. He glanced over toward his tall aide—still holding up the wall—and Julie saw some silent girl-watcher's signal pass between them. While she found that somewhat flattering, she didn't like the term *grounded* —as if women were merely flighty butterflies who needed to be brought back down to earth.

"What are you?" Fowler then asked her. "One of those kooky women's libbers?"

Julie pressed her lips together. It seemed that today everyone had a ready supply of labels. Because she had hinted at racial prejudice, Ellen Gray had wanted to know if she was a civil rights nut. Now, simply because she was not married, Alderman Paddy Fowler was ready to brand her a women's libber. She wondered what else he might call her if he knew about her involvement with the blacks and Hispanics.

"I believe in God, the flag, motherhood and apple pie, Mr. Fowler," she said, sitting erect, as if ready to leave. "And if you'll quit beating around the bush and get to the point, I just might believe in aldermen, too."

"Oh, cool down," said Fowler with a wave of his

45

hand. But, he was grinning, as if amused by her little outburst, as if it only confirmed his earlier opinion of her.

"I'm just trying to find out what we're dealing with here," the alderman explained. "If we had a frustrated housewife, there'd probably be a neglected husband—or maybe even some kids—fouling things up."

"What things?"

"And if it was a man-hating feminist, she'd probably resent some male chauvinist politico calling the shots."

"What shots?" Julie asked again. And again to no avail.

Fowler reached into his breast pocket for a fresh cigar. He slowly peeled off its cellophane wrapper. "Just how far are you willing to go," he finally asked, "to save that lousy library?"

Julie ignored the word *lousy,* filing it away with Brannigan's *old dump,* as descriptions of the McDonough Mansion by people who had no sense of either aesthetics or history.

"Whatever it takes," she answered the alderman. "Whatever will work."

"Even getting arrested again?" said Fowler.

And again Julie's mouth hung open several seconds before she was able to phrase a reply. "You mean they'd arrest me—for simply appearing before the city council?"

'Forget that," said Fowler, with a wave of his unlit cigar. "I've got something a little more dramatic in mind."

Dramatic? thought Julie. She had almost landed in jail with her first "protest." How dramatic could you get?

"Like what?" she asked the alderman.

Fowler bit off the tip of his cigar. "Like maybe dumping a load of library books on the sidewalk at City Hall."

"You're kidding," said Julie.

She watched as he lit his cigar and took a deep drag on it. Behind the puff of smoke there was a devilish gleam in his eyes. He *wasn't* kidding.

"You mean *all* of them—the whole seven thousand?"

Fowler shook his shaggy head. "A thousand should do it." He worked the cigar into a comfortable corner of his mouth. "We'll have somebody make a big sign: 'NEW SITE—MIDTOWN BRANCH LIBRARY. OPEN 24 HOURS A DAY'."

In her mind Julie could see it all: The sidewalk, the books, the big sign. The mischief-loving school girl still inside told her it was a terrific idea.

"But how would we do it?" she asked, unaware that by the use of "we" she was all but putting her blessing on the councilman's crazy scheme.

"We wait until dark," said Fowler. "Maybe two, three in the morning. We use an unmarked truck, couple strong men to unload—shouldn't take more than five or ten minutes."

"And just where would *I* fit in?" said Julie.

"You'd have to pack up the books, of course," said the alderman, switching the cigar to the other side of his mouth. "You'd also be at your desk the next morning—nine A.M. sharp—right on the sidewalk in front of City Hall."

"Oh, great!" said Julie. She amended her earlier mental vision. Now, along with the books and the sign, there was also a squad car in the picture. "For that, I ought to get about ten *years!*"

"We'll take care of that," said Fowler with a glance at Whittaker, still lounging against the wall and casually studying his fingernails. "Same as we did today."

"Then I'm as good as behind bars," said Julie. "I can't hope to be bailed out by a cop a *second* time."

"By a what?" said Fowler.

"Policeman. The very one who arrested me."

Fowler sharply glanced over at Whittaker who pulled himself off the wall to shrug his apology. "Didn't make it in time," he said sheepishly. "Got caught in traffic."

"Sure," said Fowler. "Spent too much time admiring yourself in that fancy suit. You're not a lawyer *yet*. Who said you had to look like the attorney general just to walk in and pay a fine?"

Julie saw Whittaker flush like a tardy schoolboy. And, from Fowler's scolding, she surmised that Bill Whittaker—despite the expensive suit and worldly airs—was just a law student, probably working parttime for Paddy Fowler to pay his tuition. . . And that fancy Cadillac—she wondered now if maybe that weren't Fowler's.

"Besides," said Whittaker defensively, "it was all backstage, in the judge's private chamber. Something fishy about the whole thing, if you ask me."

Fowler gave him a look that plainly said he *wasn't* asking him. All he had wanted were results, not excuses. And Julie couldn't help feeling a bit sorry for Bill Whittaker who, despite his sophisticated mien, was reduced to nothing more than a messenger boy.

"Anyway," said Fowler, turning back to Julie, "that's the whole idea. You for it or not?"

Julie's mind ran a swift replay of her earlier single-

48

handed protest—the children's innocent enthusiasm about being in a parade, her arrest by Brannigan, her behind-the-scenes trial in the judge's chamber, her agony alone in the chamber, waiting to be hauled off to jail. In the background of the little scenario was the judge's nagging question: *You didn't know such things are against the law?*

"Do I have to give you my answer right now?" she finally asked the alderman.

"It wouldn't hurt," said Fowler. "March is practically over, and I don't think you'd want to be out on the sidewalk offering curb service, singing 'April Showers'."

Julie wasn't sure she wanted to again be out on the sidewalk at City Hall—doing *anything*. "Can I at least sleep on it?"

"Sure," said Fowler. He handed her one of his business cards from a lopsided stack beside his ashtray. "I'll be here tomorrow at eight."

CHAPTER 4

"WATCH OUT FOR ALL THOSE CARTONS back there," Julie cautioned the two women. Sarah Brown and Maria Sanchez had come into the library together and were now heading for the rear of the old house. The regular Wednesday morning co-op cooking class was held—where else?—in the big room that had once served the McDonough Family as kitchen.

Her first day on the job, Julie had been surprised to find the kitchen had been left intact, with sink, stove, cupboards, and countertops. But it also warehoused an old mimeograph machine, cartons of toilet tissue, paper towels, Dixie cups, light bulbs, mimeo and typing paper, typewriter ribbons, and index cards. Other items, no longer used in an officially condemned library, were there, too. All those index cards, for instance. With no new books coming in, no new cards had to be added to the dog-eared card catalog.

But soon after Ellen Gray had left for her greener pastures, Julie had begun making some changes at the McDonough Mansion. The first was to move her librarian's desk out of the butler's pantry into the main reading room—behind the checkout desk—where she could see and be seen. The next and more arduous step was emptying the big kitchen of its boxed cargo and then neatly storing all the office and washroom supplies in the now-empty pantry.

Julie hadn't been sure then why she was emptying the kitchen, but perhaps the idea of a cooking class had already been simmering in the back of her mind. All she had been aware of st the time was a disheartening air of alienation between the blacks and Latinos who came to the library—many of them because there wasn't anywhere else to go; some of them because the temperature was more comfortable. The adults expressed their mutual distrust in either suspicious glances or total avoidance of eye contact. The children's tactics were more open—name-calling and fist fights—which resulted in the refereeing Ellen Gray had predicted.

The children were the first targets of Julie's attempts at bridging the suspicion-spawning cultural gap. She began a bilingual afternoon story hour upstairs in the children's reading rooms, reading a paragraph first in English and then in Spanish, all the while marveling at God's mysterious ways. She had never known before why she had taken six years of Spanish courses. Before long, the story hour evolved into a language class. The black children learned some Spanish and the Latinos learned a good bit of English, and all of them apparently had a good time.

Not that it all went smoothly at first. There were at

least two weeks of disruptive student exchanges—punching and elbow-jabbing—until Julie laid down the rule, in both languages, that anyone guilty of the least hostile or aggressive act toward another child would forfeit the privilege of attending the story hour for a whole week.

When the story hour had logged a successful six-month run, Julie got the idea of the Midtown Puppet Theater. At least twice a week the story hour became a puppet workshop, where the children made felt-yarn-and-button hand puppets. Later, with the checkout desk as the "stage," they used them to act out "The Mystery in Santa's Workshop"—Julie's own bilingual minidrama—as a Christmas surprise for their parents.

The puppet show was a huge success, mostly because of audience interaction. Hostilities and aloofness vanished with the children huddled together like cubs-in-a-tub behind the checkout desk, missing cues and muffing lines in each other's language.

After that, the Midtown Puppet Theater presented a new show (which meant a new story by Julie) every three months. More importantly, when Julie announced a Friday night English-as-a-second-language class, more than half of the show-watching Hispanic parents signed up.

Six of those students later became United States citizens, an event that was celebrated at the McDonough Mansion with an ethnic potluck supper—spicy Spanish dishes and succulent soul food—that would have impressed even the self-made Irish millionaire who had built the place. It was the potluck supper that inspired the co-op cooking class, another means of encouraging the black and Latino women to share their recipes on a regular basis.

As the cooking class became a regular event, Julie saw a deep, almost sisterly, bond developing between the aproned women—something she seriously doubted would ever have happened in the isolated apartment confines of the midtown ghetto.

It was also in those informal kitchen-table classes that the Spanish women learned the most practical English—words and phrases not found in any textbook, colorful idioms with which everyday American speech is so generously salted.

Julie herself helped supply some of this "salt." Licking her fingers after quickly devouring two of Maria Sanchez's chopped-liver tacos, Julie had no trouble interpreting either the English or Spanish remarks.

"You've done yourself proud, honey," smiled Sarah Brown.

Maria Sanchez, not exactly a heavyweight, herself, exclaimed, "*Dios te bendigas! El pequeno pajaro tiene much hambre!*" God bless her! The little bird has a big appetite.

"That really hit the spot," Julie had smilingly acknowledged. A good ten minutes of verbal Spanish and English juggling was required before the bewildered Latino lady smilingly nodded her understanding.

But as time went on, it was the ladies themselves and the story-hungry ghetto children who "hit the spot" with Julie. And that spot was somewhat higher than her stomach. Julie now loved each and every black or tan face, the warm, moist hands, those big dark eyes, so full of trust.

Today, many of those eyes—children's and adults' alike—held sad, questioning looks. Especially with all those cardboard cartons of books now crowding the big kitchen.

"No," Julie tried to assure them, "we're not being kicked out yet. These books are for something special."

Julie wasn't sure at what point she had agreed to Paddy Fowler's sidewalk "book blitz" or whether she had ever actually said yes. For one thing, she had not called Fowler back the morning after their first meeting in his office. And that had really been Bill Whittaker's fault for keeping her out late. After leaving the alderman's office Bill had suggested stopping off somewhere for dinner. "Somewhere" had proven to be one of the posh eateries on Michigan Avenue. From there they had gone to see a stage play at the Schubert.

And then, before she realized what was happening, Bill's dropping by the library just at closing each night to take her out to dinner had become a regular thing. And somewhere along the line Julie had begun slowly packing up the least-read books at the Midtown Branch Library.

Sarah Brown, wearing her Wednesday morning cooking class apron, now came out of the library kitchen "You want to sample the world's best refried beans and mustard greens, honey? Or you got another date with Mr. Tall-Dark-and-Loaded?"

Julie knew she meant Bill Whittaker. And maybe the expensive car *was* his, after all. But if he could afford a Cadillac, Julie wondered, why would he need to work part-time for Paddy Fowler?

"Yes and no," she answered Sarah. "Yes, I would like some beans and greens—and no, I haven't any date tonight."

Which really wasn't true. Although Bill was not

coming by to take her out to dinner, she did have a date with him—and two other men—much later that night, long after the library would close for the day. Tonight was "Operation Sidewalk"—the night Paddy Fowler's men were to dump the load of books on the sidewalk at City Hall.

She promptly closed the library at nine and then settled down at her desk to wait for Bill Whittaker and his two classmates. And just as promptly she began having doubts about her part in the alderman's scheme to set up curb service in front of City Hall.

As a Christian, could she justify such actions? Was it valid to again cite Jesus' overturning the tables of the money-changers? Or was that just a convenient cop-out? Might it not also be merely rationalizing, to compare her actions with those of Gandhi and Martin Luther King in carrying out their policies of passive or nonviolent resistance?

On the other hand, wasn't it her moral obligation to fight injustice? Wasn't it unjust to demolish a building needed by the less fortunate so others could have a speedier route to and from the jobs that kept them more fortunate? Wasn't it also unjust to destroy an old mansion rather than preserve it for future generations to study and enjoy? Or were all her protests simply Julie Chambers' means of finally getting even with the system for having bulldozed Grandma's house?

No. At least she hoped not. But because she was not really sure, Julie leaned heavily on what she was trying to accomplish at the library to ease the gnawing doubts that her motives might be less than lofty.

Not the least of her efforts to aid the disadvantaged

families of the ghetto was helping the men in those families find work. This involved her devouring the weekend want ads and then, on Monday morning, interpreting them for the jobless Latinos, often writing out directions in her own textbook Spanish. Sometimes she even made jokes about her little private non-profit "employment agency."

But this and all her other library programs—not the building or the books—was the true driving force behind Julie's quarrel with the city over the old McDonough mansion. With the closing of the Midtown Branch Library would come the end of all her meager efforts to help its patrons—children of God whom she would forever refuse to think of as either "alien" or "foreign."

While she was at her desk in the main reading room—agonizing over the rightness of her involvement with Operation Sidewalk—Julie kept glancing toward the big bay window, hoping maybe it would snow, or at least rain, so the operation would be called off and she could go home like any law-abiding librarian. No such luck. It seemed that March, having been a lamb from the start, did not intend to go out like a lion.

And then she would start in all over again, mentally weighing the pros and cons of her part in Alderman Paddy Fowler's midnight madness. It was in one of her most doubtful moments that the telephone on her desk loudly jangled. Julie hoped it might be Bill—or even Paddy Fowler—calling to say the operation was off.

She picked up the receiver after the second ring. "This is the library."

"This is the Police Department." The voice was hauntingly familiar. "Julie?"

"Yes—"

"This is Terry. Terry Brannigan."

"Oh!"

She hoped the school-girlish quickening of her pulse wasn't echoed in her voice. With a solid week of attention from someone as good-looking as Bill Whittaker, you'd think a girl wouldn't think twice about a puckish red-haired cop. But she had, every time she had passed the police station, every time she had seen a squad car.

"What time are you through over there?" he now asked.

"I'm—working late tonight."

"How late?"

"*Quite* late. In fact—" She stopped just short of telling him she probably wouldn't get through until morning. What if he had gotten wind of what was planned for tonight? What if he were just fishing for more information? Why else had he called? Julie's mind struggled through a maze of possibilities, one of which she momentarily savored and then quickly discarded: That Terry Brannigan might simply be calling because he was a guy and she was a girl.

"Why did you call, Terry?"

"I always keep tabs on pretty girls I've pinched."

He meant "arrested," of course. Now she knew he was calling about the hundred dollars he had blown in bailing her out. That was reason enough for any guy to call a girl—even this late at night.

"If it's about the money," she told him, "you'll get it on payday."

"A lot can happen between now and payday."

Julie's heart began racing again—only this time it had nothing to do with the sound of his voice. He *did* know about tonight!

"Just what do you mean by that?" she demanded.

"Just small talk."

"Well, I'm too busy for small talk, Terry."

"At eleven o'clock at night?"

"As I said—I'll drop the money off at the station on payday." And with that, she hung up.

But, for the next half hour Julie couldn't quell the suspicion that Terry Brannigan had called, not as a worried moneylender, but as a police officer on the scent of some extracurricular library activities on his beat.

. . . You didn't know such things are against the law?

Once again that nagging courtroom question crept into her mind. And Julie was right back where she had started in examining her Christian conscience. Eventually she was so sunk in a little quagmire of doubt that she didn't hear the rumble of thunder or the sudden pelt of rain on the big bay window. She *did* hear the telephone, though, and this time she caught it right after the first ring.

"Look, Terry—"

"Terry? Terry who?" asked Bill Whittaker.

"Oh, Bill! Sorry—I thought it was somebody else."

"Obviously." Was that a note of surprise in his voice? What had he thought—that no other guys ever called Julie Chambers? "I'm sure you know why I'm calling."

"Not really."

"Have you looked out the window lately?"

"Oh." Julie glanced toward the bay window. And now she both saw and heard the rain against the glass. Actually it sounded more like sleet. "That's too bad," she said, barely disguising the relief in her voice; relief, because she was sure even Paddy Fowler wouldn't take a chance on damaging city property by letting a thousand library books sit out in the rain.

"Of course, the operation is off for tonight," said Bill.

"Of course," she replied, again trying to mask her relief. She wondered if she shouldn't tell him about her other call—her suspicion that a certain policeman might somehow be wise. But she quickly decided against it. Maybe because she wasn't sure Terry Brannigan *was* wise. Or maybe because she resented Bill Whittaker's smug assumption that he was the only man in her life.

"Fowler said to sit on it." said Bill. "This stuff looks like it's turning to snow."

"Oh, fine. No more buses—and now a blizzard. How am I supposed to get home?"

"I'll be there in ten minutes," he told her.

CHAPTER 5

ONCE AGAIN CHICAGO'S CAPRICIOUS WEATHER had made April fools of its dwellers, dumping foot-and-a-half snowdrifts on their doorsteps as most of them slept, secure in their belief that it was spring. For a full day the Windy City lay paralyzed under a heavy blanket of white while its fleet of retired snowplows was slowly roused into action.

Julie Chambers was one of thousands who did not make it to work that day. Sipping a second cup of hot coffee—a rarity on any weekday morning—she sat by her front window admiring the sugary drifts. She was grateful for the unexpected holiday, determined to use it in simply lolling about the large lakeshore apartment, and in trying to get her jumbled thoughts in order.

With Operation Sidewalk so forcibly postponed, Julie wondered if the untimely blizzard had not been a bit of divine sabotage—God's way of thwarting Paddy Fowler's crazy book-dropping scheme; a sign to Julie that she should indeed sit on it—permanently.

But, how could she be *sure?* How could anyone really be sure of what God did or didn't want a person to do?

She wished she could be like some other Christians she knew whose ability to interpret God's signs, seemed to come so readily; whose walk with the Lord seemed so confident. Julie recognized that never once in her life had she ever really walked, but rather always seemed to be running. If ever there might be a sign from God—even a simple stop sign—she would probably speed right by.

When she had left Kansas for Chicago, had she gotten down on her knees and asked God if that was the right thing to do? Had she even consulted Him about going to college?

Maybe God's plan had been to humble Julie Chambers among the cornhusks, sanctify her amid the straw. But if God had wanted her to stay down on the farm, why had he given her a talent for writing? Surely not to rewrite a farmer's almanac!

With a loud sigh, Julie ended her front-window reverie and headed for the kitchen with her empty coffee cup. That was another thing she had to think about—the apartment. So wrapped up in her work at the library, she had been postponing the question of whether or not she should again advertise for someone to share the roomy apartment. And if not, just how long she would be able to go on paying the rent and utilities with her meager "library aide" salary from the city.

Taking the third-floor apartment in one of the older uptown buildings along Lake Michigan's scenic shore had been another of her "temporary" arrangements.

She had planned later—after she got her high-paying dream job on Michigan Avenue—to move into one of the many modern highrises farther south along the shore. As it was, she was a good distance from that illustrious avenue; farther still from the famous Chicago Loop. The seven-block strip of older office buildings and department stores had gotten its name because of the elevated tracks that made a loop, in which an inbound el-train immediately became outbound. Julie had heard the trains would be routed somewhat differently once the new expressway was completed, but that wouldn't in any way affect the daily travel of the Midtown Branch librarian.

Julie came downtown via the outer-drive bus which traveled south along the lakeshore and then swung onto Michigan Avenue, passing the quaint limestone water tower (at least *that* was still standing) and then eventually the big Wrigley building—poised like a huge white wedding cake at the river's edge.

Immediately after, the bus would cross the Michigan Avenue Bridge. That is, if the drawbridge was not up. Once in a while her bus would wait a good ten minutes to let a tiny tugboat and its clumsy barge pass from the murky Chicago River into the somewhat cleaner waters of Lake Michigan for its eventual voyage to ports unknown.

Julie was always fascinated by the poky yet powerful little tugboat. So much so, that during one of her drawbridge waits she had begun scribbling on an envelope what had ended up as a typewritten story entitled "Tugboat Tommy." She read it aloud to the children at the library the next day, and then, because they begged her for more, she had written a whole series—seven so far. The plot for number eight had been hastily sketched out on a notepad the last morning the outer-drive bus had had to wait for the Michigan Avenue bridge to come back down.

Once over the bridge, the bus did not turn into the Loop but went on down the avenue, Chicago's Magnificent Mile of expensive boutiques, travel agencies, and small elegant restaurants. It was along this sparkling strip that Julie got off the bus, allowing it to wend its way through the traffic without her, passing Grant Park with its concrete bandshell and fabulous Buckingham Fountain, and going on to sights yet unseen by Julie, simply because she had never taken any bus that far south.

Walking into and out of the Loop, Julie caught a westbound bus for a somewhat shorter ride that took her within walking distance of the Midtown Branch Library.

Even after three years, Julie never made the early-morning trip that she didn't feel as if she were stepping from one world to another, keenly aware of the sudden, almost shocking difference—factories, junkyards, foundries, garbage heaps, burned-out warehouses, and abandoned apartment buildings, only a few blocks west of Michigan Avenue. Before some clever word merchant had come up with the term *Magnificent Mile,* the city's oldtimers had coined another less reverent, but perhaps more realistic, phrase. To them, Michigan Avenue was merely "lace trim on a pair of dirty underpants."

In the very seat of that dirty underwear lay what was now known as the midtown ghetto. Once, before the World War II, it had been a thriving, well-kept community of Irish and Italians, many of them immigrants. Later, big defense plants had begun to lure workers out to the western suburbs into hastily built homes erected during the post-war building boom.

When the ghetto had been a neighborhood, one's landlord might be just that—a neighbor—not some phantom slumlord basking in the Florida sunshine, fanning himself with monthly rent checks from unseen tenants. If the buildings were falling apart; if the heat and the plumbing were shot, what did *he* care?

Every once in a while Julie would read in the morning paper about a number of families who had lost their homes in a fire during the night. Tragically some of them were no longer in need of any earthly home. When Julie saw headlines like that, her heart would sink, and she would anxiously scan the list of injured or dead, praying that none of her people were on the list. She wouldn't be completely satisfied until sooner or later she saw all of them at the library.

Today, sipping hot coffee in the warmth of her own roomy apartment, Julie couldn't help thinking about the impoverished families who inhabited the midtown ghetto. Many of them lived in black, soot-silted shacks that a farmer might think twice about keeping his hogs in. Some of them were on a daily diet of popcorn because they couldn't afford anything more. Others burned their furniture because the heat had been turned off.

Suddenly all her small efforts at the library seemed paltry, as if she had merely been throwing crumbs to people who really needed the whole loaf. Was she sending those poor workers into jobs where they would be further exploited?

Still steeped in such gloomy thoughts, Julie started at the ringing of the bedroom telephone.

"What's going on out there?" her father, calling from Florida, wanted to know.

"What do you mean?" said Julie, fearing he might finally have seen that news story about her arrest.

"What do I *mean*?" said her father. "Buried under a ton of snow and you want to know what I *mean*?"

"Oh, that," Julie laughed. "We're just having Christmas in April."

"Hello, Julie," said her mother, obviously on an extension elsewhere in their yet unseen condominium, "How are you, dear?"

"Fine, Mom, just fine."

"When are you coming down to visit us?"

"I'd like an answer to that, too," said her father. "We've been down here over a year now."

"Well, I couldn't come now, Dad—not with the airport all snowed under."

"That stuff won't last," he said. "Probably be gone in two days."

You don't know Chicago, Julie thought. Aloud, she said, "I'll probably come down sometime in June. After the library's closed."

"You mean they're finally going to close it?" asked her mother.

"Don't you believe it," said her father. "She's been saying that for the past three years."

"But this time it's for real," said Julie, putting into words her gut-level doubt that anything she or Paddy Fowler might do would save the McDonough Mansion.

"Any good prospects in sight?" asked her mother.

"Prospects?" said Julie. She suddenly saw a replay

of her parents' reluctantly seeing her off at the airport three years ago—the starry-eyed farmer's daughter going off to conquer the world. "You mean the media."

"No, dear. I don't mean the media."

"Oh." Julie made a small exasperated face. Her mother meant a man. And shouldn't she have known? Did her parents ever call that there wasn't the inevitable probe into Julie Chambers' love life?

"Sure," said Julie. "This place is crawling with good-looking guys. Even the cops are gorgeous."

"Cops?" said her father. "What do you know about cops?"

"You'd be surprised," said Julie. "Don't worry," she assured her mother. "When I find the right man, you'll be the first to know. And I won't have to use the telephone."

"Well, I just hope you haven't set your sights *too* high," said her mother. "You don't want to be *too* choosy."

Since when? Julie wondered.

She could hardly believe that such a remark had come from Paula Chambers who had so indelibly impressed upon her daughter the importance of being careful in choosing her lifetime mate—none other than a staunch, church-going Christian. Julie's father, of course, would have seen the right man as an industrious Kansas-born farmer. Her mother's lowering of her own sights could mean only one thing—she was afraid they might have an old maid on their hands.

In Julie's earliest years, well-meaning yet thoughtless relatives—aunts and uncles—had sadly shaken their heads at the scrawny little sparrow with which

66

God had blessed Peter and Paula Chambers. The only one who seemed to have any hope—and give Julie any hope—was her grandmother. Grandma would take Julie on her lap, hug her and whisper, "Never you mind, Sweetie. Good things always come in small packages."

But, fifth-grade boys did not know this, and the names they had thrown at her—"Toothpick," "Skinny" and "Bones"—had left deep scars, which perhaps still lay just beneath the surface of Julie's carefully constructed mid-twenties mask.

Somewhere between the ages of eleven and twelve some metamorphic miracle had taken place, and Julie had suddenly found herself no longer scrawny. In fact, her physical development suddenly was far ahead of the other girls her age. The names she was then taunted with, though totally different, were no less painful. The boys in high school had admired her brazenly, but they soon backed off from the sharp tongue she had earlier developed as a verbal shield against cutting remarks.

That was when Julie had first begun writing. Hiding away in her father's hayloft, she poured all her adolescent misery onto the pages of her daily diary, something she continued until she was eighteen.

In college, the deadly combination of her smart mouth and equally sharp mind did little to nourish any romantic possibilities. And by then, there was no man who could have measured up to her standards, anyway.

For along with her intimate writing in her father's hayloft, Julie also had done a lot of reading—countless Gothic novels from the drugstore, as well as the Bible and other inspirational books borrowed from the town library.

And it was then she had dreamily created the heroic knight in shining armor who would someday capture her heart—a thoroughly virile, yet virginal, composite of St. Francis of Assisi, Michael the Archangel, and Billy Graham.

He still lived in her mind, the model by which Julie measured any man who might want to marry her. And, for all his virtues, he most certainly would *not* be a farmer.

CHAPTER 6

AS HER FATHER HAD PREDICTED. Chicago's surprise April snow melted like fat in a hot skillet. And it wasn't long before Julie again found herself waiting at her desk one night for Fowler's boys to show up at the library in a borrowed truck for phase one of Operation Sidewalk.

They came about midnight—Bill Whittaker and two of his law school classmates. It took them only ten minutes to load the cartons of books, along with Julie's desk and chair, onto the truck. They then sat in the library kitchen drinking coffee until it was time for phase two.

Fowler had cautioned them against making the book drop too early, as some cruising patrolman was sure to discover the strange sidewalk delivery. And anyone could easily determine the source of the shipment—all he had to do was open a carton and read the library stamp inside the first book. What the officer *wouldn't* know was whether there was anything illegal about the shipment. And with the entire city asleep—City Hall itself not open until nine—there was no way he could find out. By that time, said Fowler, Julie would be behind her desk with her open-air library open for business.

Waiting for the right time to arrive, Julie also sat at the opposite end of the kitchen table, working on the latest of her "Tugboat Tommy" stories. Every now and then she had to stop writing to make another pot of coffee, each one a bit stronger than the last, for herself and her fellow conspirators, hoping the caffeine would be enough to keep her awake for the operation. Although she had made herself a hamburger for supper, it didn't occur to her that she hadn't made any plans for breakfast.

About two o'clock the men suddenly began arguing as to who was going to drive the borrowed truck over to city hall. One of Bill's classmates insisted that the driver should stay behind the wheel with the motor running—in case a quick getaway might be necessary. Bill argued that this would leave only two guys to unload their illicit cargo, stretching the delivery time out by at least five minutes.

"Ten minutes is risky enough," said Bill. "Fifteen is asking for it."

"Yeah," nodded one of the other guys. "If we're caught in the act, we won't have to worry about passing our bar exams—we'll be *behind* bars."

The argument went on for a good ten minutes, until Julie set down her ballpoint pen and said, "*I'll* drive. I was driving a truck when I was a teen-ager." Many times, back on her father's farm, she had driven into town on some errand or taken a load of produce into market.

Bill Whittaker stared at Julie for several moments and then turned to his classmates. "I don't know—what do *you* think?"

"Why not?" one of them shrugged. "That certainly solves the problem of a quick getaway."

"And with three of us unloading," said the other, "we could maybe make the drop in *less* than ten minutes."

Bill silently stared at Julie again and then finally agreed. "O.K.—you can drive. But only if I'm in the cab with you."

"Fine. I'm not *that* good a driver."

Moments later, Julie realized she had made the understatement of the year. Beside Bill in the cab of the truck, she realized it had been over three years since she had driven a car with automatic transmission, much less a truck. Now she felt as if she were missing a foot. Where *was* that stupid clutch?

She could hear Bill's two classmates in the back of the truck, loudly groaning each time she tried to get the loaded vehicle moving.

"Hey, Whittaker, take over before she strips those gears!"

"Yeah! I promised to bring this baby back in one piece!"

"Oh, *cool it!*" Bill bawled back at them. "Give her a *chance!*"

After three more unsuccessful tries, Julie finally got her bookmobile rolling.

"*Attagirl!*" she heard from behind.

She then had to listen to at least two miles' worth of jokes about lady truck drivers and the Teamsters' Union.

As Paddy Fowler had predicted, the streets near City Hall were deserted. That is, if you didn't count the two stray dogs and one staggering drunk crossing against the light.

There was something almost eerie about the empty streets, tall dark buildings and closed shops—like one of those after-the-final-holocaust movies in which two or three survivors find they are the only people left on earth.

"This is going to be a breeze," said Bill, obviously pleased with the whole setup. But suddenly a glance in the rear-view mirror brought forth an oath.

"What's wrong?" asked Julie.

"Take a look."

Julie glanced into the mirror. "Oh—*no!*" A white squad car swung out of an alley and pulled alongside them, red lights flashing.

"Pull over," the officer ordered through his speaker.

Julie obediently pulled the truck over to the curb and rolled down her window. "What's the trouble, officer?"

Terry Brannigan glanced over at Bill beside her and then opened his black book. "Ten miles over the limit."

"You're crazy!" protested Bill.

"Her word against mine," said Brannigan.

"Mine's in there, too," said Whittaker. "That makes it two against one."

Brannigan thought for a moment. "Maybe I *am* mistaken. But, there's something I'm willing to stake my life on . . . " He looked directly at Julie. "This sweet little gumdrop doesn't have a driver's license."

Julie sucked in her breath. It was true! Having

72

neither the need nor the money for a car in the city, she had never bothered to renew her driver's license. She made a hasty mental note to take care of that as soon as possible.

She also made another totally irrelevant but irresistible note. He *was* gorgeous! There should be a law against any policeman's being that beautiful.

"Tell you what, Cinderella," Brannigan said, resting his arm on the open window, "you take your coach back to the castle like a good little girl and I'll forget the whole thing."

"Nothing doing," said Bill. "*I'll* drive."

"Listen, Prince Charming," Terry said to Julie's co-pilot, "I know *exactly* what you're all up to. Either you and your chums take your cargo back to the library, or I'll pull you all into the station."

"For what?" said Bill.

"Possession of stolen property."

With that, Bill sat back on the seat, acknowledging defeat.

"Why are you doing this, Terry?" Julie asked him as he closed his black book and shoved it into his back pocket.

"A policeman's job includes the *prevention* of crime. That means stopping it *before* it happens." He looked directly into her eyes, a look that made her heart almost flip over. "Besides, I've got an investment in you."

"I told you before," she barely recognized her own voice, "I'll square up with you on payday."

"How are you going to do that if you're in *jail?*"

"Yeah, I know the one," said Paddy Fowler in his smoke-filled inner sanctum the next day. "Wouldn't think twice about pinching his own grandmother."

The alderman had summoned both Julie and Bill to his storefront office so he could get an account of the previous night's fiasco.

"What I'd like to know," said Julie, "is how he found out."

"So would I," said Fowler. He turned to Bill, who now had his head bent over one of his law books. "Who were the boys, Bill?"

"Fanelli and Fishman."

Julie almost laughed. It sounded more like a vaudeville team than a couple of struggling law students.

"Nice going, Dumbo," said Fowler. "Fanelli's the cop's *cousin*."

"How was *I* to know?" said Bill.

"I *pay* you to know!"

Julie now understood the argument back at the library about who was going to drive the truck. It was really so the one doublecrossing classmate could sneak out the back of the truck. She wouldn't be a bit surprised if he had been driven home in his cousin's squad car.

"Well, never mind," said Fowler, relighting his cigar. "There's more than one trick in the bag."

While Julie was waiting for Paddy Fowler's next trick to materialize, Mother Nature was performing some breathtaking feats of her own. Julie saw the curtain slowly rising on the springtime magic every weekday morning on her bus trip down Lakeshore Drive.

The stretch of parkway grass that rimmed the beach was turning the same green as the cellophane straw in the Easter baskets in the Michigan Avenue shop windows. The lake itself—a churning, uninviting gray during March—now reflected bluer skies. And the previously ice-capped wooden piles of the breakwater had become momentary perches for feathered friends who had either been in hiding for the winter or had just come back from their yearly vacation down south.

Even more delightful to Julie was April's handiwork at the old McDonough estate. The surrounding lawn had become a coverlet of the same lush Easter-basket green, tufted here and there with a random nosegay of violets and an occasional defiant yellow dandelion. Fresh green sprouts at the foundation of the old building signaled yet another resurrection—the coming to life of the perhaps century-old ivy that, by June, would have woven a green leafy network over the red bricks of the McDonough mansion.

Even more certain evidence of the arrival of spring was the gradual disappearance of outdoor clothing from the wall hooks in the building's front foyer. Or could it be that fewer people were coming to the library these days?

If so, Julie could hardly blame them. She was sure all of her people knew that June would bring something more than just summer. With the library windows open every afternoon to let in the April breeze, you couldn't help hearing the grind and crunch of the bulldozers but a few blocks away. Already one of the city's oldest churches had fallen victim to the swinging steel ball of the wrecker's crane, with the resulting rubble now being scooped up by the bulldozers, dumped into trucks, and then hauled off to some abandoned quarry out in the suburbs.

Julie knew the old church had long been without a

congregation. But, if a beautiful old limestone landmark like that wasn't to be spared, how could she
expect anything better for an old red-brick mansion?
The thought truly depressed her.

Equally depressing were the boxes of undelivered
Operation Sidewalk books, again crowding the library
kitchen. And now there were new stacks of flattened
cardboard cartons to be filled with the remainder of
the books that had made a library out of the old
McDonough mansion.

By the middle of May, Julie had given up on Paddy
Fowler's ability—or perhaps even his interest—in
coming up with some trick to save the library. But Bill
continued to assure her his boss was still thinking.

Then the long-dreaded telephone call came. Julie
was to start packing. It seemed that with the absence
of the usual April rains, construction on the expressway was ahead of schedule. During the brief conversation Julie also finally learned the destination of the
Midtown Branch's total cache of books. They were to
be sent downtown and integrated into those already
on the shelves of the main library.

Glumly, Julie hung up the phone. Because it was
her lunch hour, the LIBRARY CLOSED sign was up
on the front door. She wondered now if she shouldn't
just leave it up permanently. No. That would surely
be admitting defeat. But *shouldn't* she admit it? The
sign on the door, the lunchtime quiet of the library,
Paddy Fowler's silence—weren't they all omens of
things to come? Wasn't her attempt to save the library
now just a lost cause?

Glancing toward the children's stairway, Julie wondered if she shouldn't take down the clock in the
children's reading room.

The clock wasn't the kind normally found in a library. A German-made cuckoo, it was her own. It had hung on the kitchen wall back home in Kansas ever since she could remember. Julie had placed it in the children's reading room shortly after Ellen Gray had left for her new job out in the suburbs.

Julie suspected her mother had given her the clock as a link to the farm—an hourly reminder to Julie Chambers that should she not make it in the big city, she was always welcome back on the farm. That paradox—the fact that her parents would spend a fortune on her college education and then hope she would stay on the farm—had always puzzled Julie.

Reluctantly her parents had seen her off on the plane for Chicago. Little had they known that before long they, too, would be leaving Kansas. Her father's farming was now limited to tending small plants on the balcony of their two-bedroom condo in St. Petersburg, and her mother's cuckoo clock was now but a reminder of days gone by.

In the silence of the now-empty library, Julie heard the clock signal the hour. As a child, she had never lost her delight at the little wooden bird's sassily springing out. As a story-telling librarian, she always enjoyed watching her small listeners eye the clock with the same childish anticipation; even more fun were their squeals of delight when she would sass the little bird back.

"Who's cuckoo?"

Julie wondered now, if she had not, in fact, become a bit "cuckoo" in trying to save the library. A professed Christian—an avowed keeper of the Commandments—how many times had she broken the civil law?

Disturbing the peace, blocking the entrance to a public building and demonstrating without a permit.

She could see him as if it had happened only that morning: the baby-faced blue-uniformed arresting officer, counting off her threefold transgressions before the tired judge.

And the night of Operation sidewalk—his muscular right arm on the truck window, his beautiful face only inches from hers: . . .

Doesn't have a driver's license . . . possession of stolen property . . . sweet little gumdrop . . .

Sweet little gumdrop? Terry Brannigan had called her *that?*

She sat for several moments, dreamily smiling at her librarian's desk, until she caught her reflection in the bay window. *Idiot!* Yes, she *had* gone off her rocker. If Terry Brannigan thought her so "sweet," why hadn't she seen him in all these weeks? Of course, he was interested in only one thing—maintaining law and order on his beat. And so long as Julie Chambers wasn't breaking the law, there was no reason for his again calling at the library.

Julie sighed and reached for her purse, deciding to walk over to the nearby greasy spoon for some lunch. But, before she got up from the desk, the telephone rang.

"Hey, babe—Fowler."

"Oh. Hello."

"Bill's on his way over for you right now. I've finally got it."

"Got what?"

"The trick to save that old mausoleum."

78

CHAPTER 7

ON HIS WAY TO PICK HER UP, Bill had stopped off for some hamburgers—their lunch—to be eaten around the desk at Fowler's office.

Between wolflike attacks on his burger, the alderman told Julie of his latest scheme to save the Midtown Branch Library. If his earlier idea about the open-air library had been crazy, this one was sheer suicide.

"You've got to be kidding," said Julie. She turned to Fowler's assistant, seeking his assurance.

But Bill shook his head. "It's no joke, Julie."

Fowler's latest scheme was for Julie—with all of her people, children included—to go out in the street the morning the wrecking crew arrived and stage a bulldozer-blocking sitdown.

"No way," said Julie.

"I thought you wanted to save the library."

"I do. But—"

"And that you have guts."

She *had* guts. But she also had a conscience, and she would never again exploit any of those innocent children. Or their parents, for that matter.

They were all silent: Fowler, beginning on his second hamburger; Bill, merely sitting in a corner with his arms folded.

"All right," she finally agreed. "I'll do it. On one condition."

"Shoot."

"That it's just me—nobody in front of the bulldozer but me."

His mouth full of hamburger, Fowler sat for a moment, studying Julie in her lemon-yellow summer shirtwaist. Then he shook his head. "No good. It's gotta be a crowd." One five-foot-three librarian could easily be dismissed as some nutty broad with a personal ax to grind. But it would be hard to ignore both the number and the motives of a whole crowd of concerned citizens.

Giving the matter some more thought, Julie knew the alderman was right. But if she did actually go through with it, she would have to make certain that the people fully understood what they would be doing. They would readily agree to it, she was sure. In fact, she could actually see two of the most willing members of the street gang—Maria Sanchez and Sarah Brown in their cooking-class aprons—shaking their wooden spoons at the wrecking crew.

"Just grownups?" she asked the alderman. "No children?"

"Just grownups," said Fowler. Having polished off his two hamburgers, he loudly sucked his teeth and then reached into his breast pocket for a fresh cigar. "A deal?"

Until then, Julie had not taken so much as a bite out of her own hamburger. Now she slowly unwrapped it. "I need some time to think about it."

"There *isn't* any time," said Fowler. "That isn't a summer breeze, baby—those are bulldozers breathing down that pretty neck."

She had just closed the library for the day and was heading for the corner mailbox when Terry Brannigan got out of his parked car. He took her by the arm and led her over to the curb.

"*Now* what?"

"Disturbing the peace again." He waited until she was settled on the front seat of the car. "*My* peace."

He closed the door, came around the front of the car, and got in behind the wheel. Before he had time to turn the key, Julie handed him a small white stamped envelope containing two fifty dollar bills— the long-promised money he had spent in bailing her out.

"This will spare me the trouble of mailing it."

Terry ignored both the envelope and her remark. "I know what you and that cigar-chewing politician have got cooked up."

She looked toward the window. "I don't know what you're talking about."

"Baloney!"

He turned the key in the ignition and pulled away from the curb. Julie completely forgot that Bill was to pick her up in front of the library.

"Anyway—how did *you* find out? Nobody was supposed to know about it."

"Are you kidding? By the time that bulldozer pulls up, you won't *have* to block it. The reporters and cameramen will do it for you."

Julie wondered: Had Fowler done that—notified the newspapers? Maybe even the TV stations? But, of course, why shouldn't he? Wasn't that the whole idea, to arouse public concern?

"Fine," she said. "That's just what we want—publicity."

"You'll get more than publicity." She was sure he meant she would be arrested again.

"That's all right, too."

Her chauffeur gave her a long look as they waited at a corner for the light to turn green. "It means that much to you?"

"Yes. I think there are some things in life more important than expressways." She punctuated her declaration by ceremoniously placing the unmailed, unaccepted white envelope between them on the front seat.

And again he ignored it. "You can't stop progress, Julie—it's a part of life."

"So is compassion. Or at least it should be."

Julie felt she had won that round, until he said, "You think I don't care about all the things you're doing at the library? I've been working with some of these ghetto kids, too, Julie, and I don't check out their color—or accent—before they walk in the door."

Her mouth dropped open in surprise.

"And the day I do, I'll not only turn in my badge, but My Christian dogtags, too. I'd be phony as a Pharisee—calling Christ my Savior and then turning my back on any one of those He died to save."

"Then what are we arguing about?" said Julie.

"I'll *tell* you what we're arguing about." But he didn't. Not until he parked the car in front of her apartment building and turned off the engine.

Julie briefly wondered how he knew where she lived—but didn't Chicago's nosiest cop know *everything?*

"When are you going to wise up, Julie?" he now asked her. "Can't you see he's just using you?"

"Who?"

"Your friendly neighborhood alderman. Who do you think is going to bail you out *this* time?"

"Naturally, not *you.*"

"Fowler—champion of the underdog. Not only a damsel in distress, but a readymade cause. I can see it on the front page: FOWLER FIGHTS TO SAVE LIBRARY."

Julie could also see it. The story would be a lot bigger than the two-inch item about her first arrest. There would probably be a picture with this story: the Midtown librarian and some of her favorite people being herded, in handcuffs, into a paddy wagon. This time it would surely make the Florida newspapers. She only hoped her father wouldn't have another heart attack.

Still, there was something about Terry Brannigan that got her own Irish up. The need to antagonize this beautiful baby-faced policeman was stronger than any aversion to again breaking the law.

"Super," she said. "Maybe I'll even write the story myself."

She could see he was having trouble suppressing a little laugh. At least that uniform hadn't completely gone to his head—he still had a sense of humor.

Terry slowly shook his head. "You're really something, Julie—you know that?"

"Is that supposed to be a compliment?"

"I didn't pick you up to hand you any bouquets, dollface."

"Why *did* you pick me up?"

He shifted on the seat, took her chin in his hand and turned her face to his. Without any trouble at all, he could have kissed her.

"Julie, if you think you're going to sit in the street to save the library, you're kidding yourself. All you'll be doing is campaigning."

Her eyes were drawn to his mouth—the way his lip puckered so temptingly over the one crooked tooth. "What do you mean—campaigning?" she heard herself ask.

"For Fowler," he said, dropping his hand. He reached across her and opened the car door. "In case you don't already know it, your fairy godfather is up for reelection this fall."

Having spent the weekend cramming for his upcoming bar exams, Monday night Bill took Julie out to the suburbs for dinner, apparently having exhausted every decent place in the city. They ate at La Villa Royale, one of those sprawling, plushly-carpeted candlelit restaurants where the clink of cocktail glasses all but drowned out the pianist.

Bill ordered their usual—filet mignon—without even bothering to open the menu. It was probably just as well. The feeble, flickering glow of the ruby-jarred candle on the table did little to illuminate the bill of fare. He also did not bother asking Julie if she would like a drink, having learned on their first date that she didn't drink. He himself seemed to have little interest in the double martini he had ordered for himself, sitting with his dark eyes down, fingering the stem of the elegant glass.

"Where were you Friday night?" he finally asked.

84

"I came by at closing and you were already gone. Weren't home, either. I thought we had a date."

"Sorry about that. But I got picked up by the police."

Bill leaned back in his chair as the waiter set his still-sizzling steak down before him. In the candlelight it was hard for Julie to read his expression. "Brannigan, no doubt."

"Like the man said—wouldn't think twice about pinching his own grandmother."

"Or stealing another guy's girl."

"Don't be silly. He only came for his money."

"Listen, Julie, I saw the way he looked at you that night in the truck." He sliced fiercely at his filet. "Behind that baby face lurks a mind just as human as the next guy's."

Julie dismissed that with a little snort. *The idea that Terry Brannigan might be interested in her!* He had been off duty when he had picked her up—he could easily have taken her out to dinner. Rather, he had left her standing at the curb, her mouth agape at his parting shot about Paddy Fowler's using her and the library simply to get reelected.

And then, because she wasn't sure Terry was wrong, she had purposely made herself unavailable to the alderman's good-looking aide. A quick bite of supper at the local snack shop preceded her stewing—through a two-hour movie—about Bill Whittaker's obvious part in her friendly neighborhood alderman's preelection scheme.

Because Bill was studying all weekend, Julie had had two full days to brood about it, and the result was that tonight her frequent dinner partner seemed like a total stranger. Every little gesture, every small compliment—the whole dinner—took on a new meaning. Now she sat across from him, unenthusiastically poking at her expensive filet as if it might have been yesterday's leftovers.

"What's wrong?" said Bill.

"Nothing," she lied.

Bill remained lost in thought for the rest of the dinner. He was quiet as he drove her home, and as they rode the elevator up to her apartment.

"Julie." He caught her hand as she turned the key in the lock. "I think it's time you and I had an understanding."

"Yes," she nodded. "I think it *is* time you leveled with me."

He withdrew his hand. "What do you mean?"

"This phony sitdown. It *is* just to get your boss reelected, *isn't* it?"

Bill opened his mouth. But the would-be barrister was speechless.

"And all this fancy dining. Just another campaign expenditure—like bumperstickers and brochures."

"You're crazy."

"Oh, come on, Bill—I went to school, too. I didn't have money for filet mignon every night of the week, or to gas up a Cadillac."

"So Fowler's footing the bill," he finally admitted. "So what?"

"So you can tell your cigar-crazy boss he can find himself another patsy—*that's* what!"

She stormed into the apartment and slammed the door.

The next morning she hung the LIBRARY CLOSED sign up on the door—permanently. She didn't think it necessary to lock the big double doors, but moments later, up on a ladder in the main reading room, emptying the top bookshelf marked "Social Science," she was sorry she hadn't. Paddy Fowler walked in.

The alderman shifted his cigar from one side of his mouth to the other, eyeing her, perched in her stocking feet midway up on the ladder. "I thought you were smart."

"I am," she said, slowly climbing down with an armful of books. "And getting smarter every minute."

He stood there, chewing on the cigar, as Julie dumped the books into one of several open-mouthed cardboard cartons on the reading table. "The cop, huh?"

"I don't need Brannigan to clue me," she bluffed, taking a charcoal pencil from behind her ear. "I can think for myself."

"And just how far do you think you're going to get—by yourself?"

"At least not in jail." Apparently he hadn't yet gotten it through his candidate's head that it was all over—that Julie Chambers was no longer fighting for a lost cause.

But maybe he had. Because now he pulled one of the chairs away from the table and sat down in what first appeared a gesture of defeat. He reached into the still-open carton on the table, took out one of the books, and glanced at the title. "You ought to read some of these books sometime. Might learn something."

Julie said nothing, taking the book from him and marking with her pencil the total number of books in the box.

"Such as how your city is run."

"I know how the city is run." *By self-serving politicians like you.*

"Then you know, of course, about the two-party system."

She put the pencil back behind her ear. "I'm sure you didn't come all the way over here just to give me a lesson in civics."

"That's where you're wrong. That's *exactly* why I came over here." He eased back in the chair, as if it might be his own back at the office. He set the dead cigar on the edge of the table. "Let's take a hypothetical case. Let's say there are—we'll make it simple—ten men on the city council. And let's assume that six of those ten are—" he paused, "we'll call them *conservative.*"

"Don't bother," she interrupted him, tearing a piece of masking tape off a roll and pressing it down to seal the cardboard carton.

"The other four—" Fowler went on, not the least bit discouraged, "are *liberal.* Now, for the conservatives, that constitutes a—"

"Majority." Julie filled in the verbal blank, moving over to the next carton.

"Good girl." The alderman leaned forward and picked up the dead cigar. He turned it over in his fingers as if it were a nut he somehow had to crack. "Now, let's assume that among the conservatives, there is one councilman who has . . . we'll call it influence, which means that this particular councilman is able, on occasion, to . . . "

"Pressure his fellow party members."

"Ah! Now you *are* getting smart."

"Look, I know all about such political shenanigans," Julie snapped, hands on hips. "What does all this doubletalk have to do with me—or the library?"

"Simply this." He took a book of matches out of his coat pocket and lit the soggy cigar. He squinted at Julie through the cloud of foul-smelling smoke.

"Let's say you *were* able to start somebody thinking that maybe it wouldn't be such a bad idea to tear up that playground"—he nodded to where the ghetto children, locked out of their library, were noisily playing on the swings and monkey bars—"and leave the library where it is."

Julie thought of her last letter to the mayor. A carbon copy had gone to the Landmark Commission. Was Fowler saying "somebody" might be thinking of preserving the old mansion as a historical landmark? Could the city be considering tearing up the playground to use for the expressway on-ramp? If that were so, then Fowler wouldn't be able to cash in on it and would lose his chance to play champion of the underdog, as Terry had so aptly put it. All his hoped-for preelection publicity would go right down the drain.

"Let's just say that is the case," said Fowler, "and that somebody draws up a resolution and it's put before the council for a vote."

Julie was sure, now, that something was brewing with the city fathers. If not, why was this particular father going to all this trouble?

"Now, here—" he said with that calculated pause again, "here is where the majority comes in. In order for the resolution to pass, it must get a majority vote. At least six of the city councilmen must vote for it."

Julie picked up a stray book and turned it over in her hands.

"What you're really saying is, if I don't go along with you on the sitdown—don't let you play the big hero—you'll squash me right on the council floor."

"Precisely. Presuming, of course, that you would be able to apply enough pressure. "

He waved the suggestion aside with his cigar as if that were the least of his worries.

"But how would that look?" she said, brushing a bit of dust from the book. "You and your party taking an outright stand against culture?" *Like a bunch of bums*, she answered herself.

From the way he frowned, turning the cigar over in his fingers, Julie was sure the alderman was thinking the same thing.

"On the other hand," he said slowly, "what arouses the public more—culture or prejudice? I can't see myself losing too many votes by exposing your cute little want-ad caper: Finding jobs for these foreigners—jobs that *should* go to *real* Americans."

Julie almost dropped the book.

"And that," he said confidently, "is the very last thing you'd want to happen. Right?"

She slammed the book down on the table. "You know what *this* is—" *Blackmail*, she intended to say.

Rising from his chair, the alderman used his own tobacco-stained word. "Politics, my dear girl—*politics*."

CHAPTER 8

SHE TOOK IT OUT on the first person she met. "What did you do—run out of grandmothers?" she snarled at Terry Brannigan who was waiting for her as she came down the library steps at the end of the day.

For the first time since she had met him, he was at a loss for words. Of course, he couldn't possibly know what she meant—what Paddy Fowler had said about whom a certain overzealous cop wouldn't hesitate "pinching."

"Put a badge on some Boy Scouts," she added, "and they think they're policemen."

"This badge," he said, finally finding his voice, "is the only thing that's saving you."

"From what?"

"A good old-fashioned spanking."

They were already a block down the street before Julie realized that, without even thinking, she had gotten into his old car.

"What did he offer you?" Terry asked her, as she sat silently fuming. "A seat on the library board?"

As usual, he knew about everything—that she had once been on the outs with Paddy Fowler, but was now again in.

"How is it you always know everything?"

"I make it my business to know. Especially when you're involved."

Knowing she was angry with no one but herself didn't keep her from needling him. "I'll bet you even sleep with it on."

"What?"

She nodded to his uniform. "That monkey suit. With your police manual tucked under your pillow."

He gave her a sidelong glance and then laughed his husky laugh. "No, as a matter of fact, I'm going to get rid of this monkey suit right now. Steiner's got a rule against Boy Scouts camping out in his garden."

It took Julie a few moments to digest that. "Oh, now wait a minute! If you think you're going to take me to some restaurant and butter me up with a two-inch steak . . . "

"On *my* salary? Hamburger—if you're lucky."

Terry parked the car in front of a large two-story stone house with a ROOM FOR RENT sign in its front window. Terry Brannigan must live alone in one of many rooms in that dismal-looking house. But why should that bother her? She wouldn't care if he lived in solitary confinement at the county jail.

And later, with him again beside her on the front seat of his car, she told herself she didn't care, either, what Terry Brannigan looked like in slacks and a sports jacket.

When he finally pulled into the alley behind the Blue Angel and its outdoor garden, Julie stubbornly sat, arms folded, until he opened the car door and gently took her by the arm. "Come on, Julie—I hate to eat alone."

It wasn't steak *or* hamburgers. It was schnitzel and noodles, served out in the *sommergarten* by Herman Steiner himself, a gravy-stained white apron tied around his broad middle.

Julie couldn't help thinking that the thickly hedged garden, with its two leafy oak trees, red-checked tablecloths and blue Chinese lanterns, was far more romantic than any of the fancy places Bill Whittaker had taken her. She thought less kindly, though, of Steiner's "blue angel" out in the center of the garden. It wasn't really an angel, but one of those corny sculpted cupids, complete with bow and arrow. And it wasn't blue—the overhead lantern just made it look blue.

Julie's dinner partner apparently noticed her nose-wrinkling appraisal of their host's taste in sculpture. "Picked it up in a junkyard," he said, nodding to Steiner, busily serving up some more weiner schnitzel—the specialty of the house—to another couple at an adjoining table.

"He should have left it there." She picked up her fork, preparing to sample her own serving. "Why in the world does he call it blue?"

"Got a thing about blue," said Terry. "Uniforms included."

He nodded to some of the other tables. And for the first time, in the dim glow of the blue lanterns, Julie noticed that almost all the other men were in uniform. In fact, the place was loaded with policemen, out with their girls.

"If he didn't," said Terry, "he'd be out of business. We're the only thing keeping him open—only ones with stomachs strong enough for Steiner's cooking."

"What are you talking about?" she said, savoring her first mouthful of breaded veal. "This stuff is delicious."

"Then eat hearty," he said, picking up his fork. "Next time it *will* be hamburgers."

Julie took another forkful and purposely concentrated on chewing the savory schnitzel, wondering at her partner's casual reference to "next time."

"You know, he actually keeps count?" said Terry.

Julie looked up from her plate. "Who?" she asked. "Count of what?"

"Steiner. How many guys end up proposing out in this garden. He thinks it's that dumb statue." He took a mouthful of noodles. "More likely it's the beer."

Only then did Julie realize they were the only couple in the garden without a pitcher of beer on their table.

"I forgot to even ask you," said Terry. "Would you like some?"

She firmly shook her head. "But you go right ahead."

"Never touch the stuff." He took another mouthful of noodles and talked right through them. "Don't get me wrong—I'm no saint. It's just that I've seen too much of what alcohol can do—especially out on the street."

Somewhere between the alley and the garden, Julie had lost her pique at the cop's "kidnapping." But that wasn't surprising. She doubted there was any woman alive who could sit across a lantern-lit table from Terry Brannigan—and stay mad at him.

In slacks and sports jacket he looked no older than he did in a policeman's uniform. She decided it was his nose—turned up at the end as if it might have been pressed too long against the glass of a candy counter.

Or maybe it was that freshly-scrubbed look, as if his mother might have just washed him behind the ears.

Or it could have been the way his lip puckered over that one crooked tooth—as if he were constantly begging for a kiss.

Whatever it was, Julie doubted he would ever lose it. He probably would apply for Medicare looking like somebody's kid brother.

And yet, despite his boyish appearance, there was something terribly male, terribly exciting about Terry Brannigan. As if there were, as Bill Whittaker had put it, more than one would suspect behind that baby face.

"What made you become a policeman, Terry?" she found herself asking during dessert.

"Like the lady said—" He took a sip of his coffee—"I really thought I was joining the Boy Scouts."

"Come on," she chided him. "Aren't you ever going to let me forget that?"

"Probably not." He set his cup down. "How did you ever get mixed up with that library?"

"Why? What's wrong with the library?"

"Nothing. Only you don't exactly fit my childhood memories of librarians."

"Oh? And just what is that?"

He made a long, somber face that left little doubt.

"There was this one old stone-faced duchess who kept tiptoeing around the tables with her finger on her lips. I thought the only word she knew was *Shhh!* "

Julie laughed, recalling a number of times she had applied the same sibilant strategy in the children's reading room at the Midtown Library.

"I was a real devil back then—"

"*Back then?*"

"But for some reason this old gal took a shine to me. Always patting me on the head."

Julie could easily visualize that. There probably still were a lot of ladies, not all of them necessarily old, who would take a shine to Terry Brannigan.

"And then I'd have to beat up half the neighborhood on my way home."

"Poor baby," she cooed mockingly. "And I suppose that's when you decided to become a policeman."

"No, I decided that when I was twelve. The night some cop came to the door to give me and my sister the bad news."

"Bad news?"

"About my parents. Killed in an auto accident."

"Oh, Terry!"

"Head-on collision. The other driver was drunk."

"Terry, I'm so *sorry*." She fought the impulse to reach across the table and lay her hand on his.

"Anyway," he went on, "he was a great big burly guy, Julie, but the way he handled us kids—gentle as a kitten. And his eyes—I'll never forget his eyes. The guy was really hurting for us. I decided that very night that's what I wanted to be. Not just a cop—but a cop like him. Somebody who could *feel* for people."

Julie thought of the first time she had sat down with Terry—on the front seat of his old car, the day they had met. Even then she had sensed that under that blue uniform he was something more than "just a cop."

"Of course, I had another motive," said Terry, "I wanted to pull every drunk driver off the street and slap him in jail. Trouble is, we don't always know who's drunk—until after they've killed somebody."

Again Julie had to fight the impulse to touch him. Instead, she said, "That must have been terrible for you—suddenly losing both your parents."

Though her own parents were many miles away—and it had been a long time since she had seen them—still she knew they were there if she ever needed them. Or they needed her.

"It wasn't exactly roses for my grandmother, either," he said with a nod. "There she was, a widow trying to make ends meet on Social Security, and suddenly she finds herself with two teenagers to raise—and one of them a grade-A punk."

"You—a *punk?*"

"Thought I was going to get away with murder," he nodded again. "But I got the surprise of my life—Grandma had a left hook like Muhammad Ali."

"You don't mean she actually *punched* you."

He grinned. "No, but I was never sure she wouldn't."

He looked down at the table then, at her hand so close to his. With a simple turn of his wrist, he was holding her hand—as it it were the most natural thing in the world.

"And you know something, Julie—when my grandmother died, I think I missed her even more than my parents. And it still bothers me that I never got around to telling her that I loved her."

When he lifted his head and looked at her, Julie knew then that his eyes were what made his face so appealing. They were full of mischief, yes. But kindness and compassion, too, and suffering. All she had earlier tried *not* to see.

He gently rubbed his thumb across her knuckles. "How did we get on *this* subject?"

"I asked you."

"Yeah, but it's hardly what I planned for our first date."

First date? Julie thought: She wasn't sure she wanted to know exactly what Terry Brannigan meant by that, wasn't sure it had been wise to ask him any questions about what made him tick. She already knew one thing. He was the first man she had ever met who had the power to break her heart. How she knew that, she wasn't sure. But she knew it.

"I think it's time you took me home, Terry."

It was with her again in his car—the feeling that she was heading for trouble, that Terry Brannigan somehow spelled heartbreak.

But wasn't she just letting her imagination run away with her? So he had taken her to dinner, shared some innermost thoughts, and even held her hand. So what? Wasn't he merely trying to change her mind about the library sitdown?

"I don't think that's really fair," he said as they pulled out of the alley.

"What isn't fair?"

"That I should spill my guts out and still not know anything abut you."

"It's just as well. You'll have less to use against me in court."

He momentarily took his eyes off the road to look at her. "Don't tell me *you* have a shady past."

"Why do you think they ran me out of Kansas on a

rail? I'm writing my memoirs right now—*Sin in a Silo.*"

He threw his head back in an appreciative laugh. She might have laughed, too, if she hadn't been so busy wondering how the evening was going to end. She had hoped that by the mention of court, she might have steered the conversation onto less personal ground. Or better yet, have started an argument.

"You're priceless, Julie." He reached over to give her hand a little squeeze. "But Kansas? You mean you grew up on a *farm?*"

She nodded.

"That's fantastic," he said, almost to himself. "Simply fantastic," as if he had, indeed, stumbled upon some priceless treasure. "I never would have guessed."

"You just never looked close enough. The big shots on Michigan Avenue did, though. They spotted the hayseed in my hair the minute I walked in the door . . ."

He looked at her questioningly, as if for some explanation.

But she only made a small face. "That's a long story—and it's really not very important anymore."

Amazingly, that was true. Somewhere along the line in the past three years, she had forgotten all about her determination to conquer the world of mass media. Which only made her wonder, now, how serious she had been to begin with.

"Well, anyway," said Terry, "don't kid yourself."

"About what?"

"About my not looking close enough."

And because he was doing that now—looking at her—the cop almost went through a red light.

Glancing about, in search of something—anything—to take her mind off her driver, Julie let her eyes rest on the well-known and much-revered Prayer of St. Francis of Assisi, scotch-taped to his sunvisor:

Lord, make me an instrument of Your peace;
where there is hatred, let me sow love;
where there is injury, pardon;
where there is doubt, faith;
where there is despair, hope;
where there is darkness, light; and where there is sadness, joy.

O Divine Master,
grant that I may not so much seek
to be consoled as to console;
to be understood, as to understand;
to be loved, as to love:
For it is in giving that we receive,
it is in pardoning that we are pardoned,
and it is in dying that we are born
to eternal life.

She might have asked him about his use of the prayer—one of her favorites—but she was still fearful of knowing too much about this irresistible man who already occupied so many of her thoughts. To give him room in her head was still harmless. To let him invade her heart would be inviting disaster.

But wasn't it already too late? Hadn't he already stolen at least half of her heart?

Going up with him in the apartment elevator, Julie had a thoroughly knee-weakening sensation. She felt as though she were falling, falling—head over heels—right over the edge of a cliff, with neither the power nor the desire to be rescued.

The feeling grew in intensity when they reached her apartment door. Terry stood with his hands in his pockets while she blindly fished around in her bag for her key.

"I hope you don't think tonight makes any difference, Terry."

"Of course not."

"We're still on opposite sides of the fence."

"Naturally."

She turned the key in the lock. "And I'm not going to ask you in."

"Certainly not." He took his hands from his pockets. "You all through now?"

"Yes—"

"Great." He took her in his arms, leaned her back against the door, and kissed her. "Good night, Julie."

CHAPTER 9

PADDY FOWLER CALLED IT a lucky break. The newspapers called it incompetence. Julie wondered if it wasn't the small library-saving miracle for which she had prayed.

She didn't know if Fowler ever got down on his well-padded knees to thank the Good Lord for anything, but after his call, she had visions of his dancing a jig over the item on the front page of the morning's Tribune:

LEGAL "OVERSIGHT" HALTS EXPRESSWAY

According to the story, while the city's engineers had been most precise in their calculations for the new expressway, someone in the large corps of civil attorneys had not completely followed through on legal condemnation procedures involving one triangular parcel of private property.

For a few days Julie entertained the naïve hope that such an oversight might totally halt construction of the new expressway. If so, Chicago might be blessed with the eighth wonder of the world, a nice concrete roadway—much like Tevye's dreamed-of rich man's stairway—leading nowhere.

But Paddy Fowler quickly sobered her up with his own probably accurate calculations that the legal red tape involving the purchase would be, at the most, several months long. That was why the alderman considered the mistake such a lucky break.

The bulldozers would probably be back to work sometime in September, and Julie's outraged citizens' sitdown—with Fowler's subsequent heroics on the council floor—would still be fresh in the minds of voters at election time.

Even more sobering was the mayor's terse typewritten reply to Julie's latest letter. The Midtown Branch librarian was to continue packing.

Sometime during the following weeks of tedious activity, Julie discovered some other well-written letters, these in a Manila file folder which had somehow slipped under the other folders she had shoved to the back of the library filing cabinet to make room for her "Tugboat Tommy" stories.

Much to her surprise, she discovered, in the folder labeled "Landmark Commission," some lengthy five-year-old correspondence between the commission and Ellen Gray. Her predecessor obviously had tried to have the library declared an historical landmark.

Thumbing through the file, Julie wondered if it were complete. Could some later correspondence have been lost or misfiled? The last communication in the handful of stapled carbons and originals was a letter from the Landmark Commission, informing Ellen Gray that they would shortly begin an investigation of

103

the McDonough Mansion to determine whether it might, in fact, be the work of a certain now-famous architect.

Julie apparently had badly misjudged the former Midtown librarian. The woman obviously was not unfeeling; was able to appreciate the historic value of a century-old mansion—even if she had called it a rat-trap. Perhaps that disparaging remark had sprung from bitterness over her post at the helm of a sinking ship.

Julie glumly put the file of letters back in the drawer. Maybe she, too, would share Ellen's attitude when it was all over. Maybe she would forever hold a grudge against a system that would so dispassionately dispose of two architectural gems—a red-brick Chicago "castle" and a lovely eight-sided Kansas homestead.

Packing up the children's books hurt most of all. Not that Julie's little dark-eyed patrons could read any but the simplest of them. The children's reading room at the Midtown Branch Library had been more than just books. It had been a quiet (well, sometimes) refuge from the clatter and clank of the city's crowded streets. Often it had provided a magic carpet ride to faraway lands where the air was always clean and the hero always won; where the children could temporarily forget about the broken windows, street gangs, rats crawling into their beds at night, and fathers who did not come home after work—simply because there was no work.

But the city that was at times their worst enemy would not leave the poor little inner-city kids totally without books. Magnanimously, the library board had decided to bless the midtown ghetto with a "traveling library"—an old beat-up bookmobile. If Julie hadn't been so depressed, the irony might have amused her. The library board had also generously offered her the job as pilot of the bookmobile, and, if she took the job, it would again be "Operation Sidewalk."

She supposed that such a job would be better than nothing. She would still have daily contact with her children, but a story hour for thirty or forty kids inside a bookmobile was out of the question.

Suddenly, as if prearranged, the little cuckoo in the clock upstairs began to sassily call the hour. Six o'clock. There was also the sharp ring of the front-desk telephone, and Julie sped down the stairs to answer it.

"I hear," said Paddy Fowler without preamble, "that you've been chasing around with that cop."

Bill, Julie thought. The brushed-off barrister had finally tattled to his boss.

She did not deny the alderman's hearsay, because it was partly true. She had been seeing a lot of Terry Brannigan, but it could hardly be called "chasing around." Most of the time it was a quick kiss either in the library kitchen or over the counter at the checkout desk—brief stopoffs by the cruising patrolman, with his squad car at the curb, engine still running.

Sometimes Julie walked the five blocks over to an old abandoned rubber factory that had been converted into a gym and where, between shifts, the Midtown policemen worked out to keep physically fit for the force that was sometimes necessary in the line of duty.

Once in a while she and Terry did actually go out—usually to Steiner's *Sommergarten* where they would stuff themselves with wiener schnitzel and, time permitting, sit and talk in the glow of Steiner's blue angel.

"I hope he hasn't changed your mind," said Fowler. He was, of course, referring to Julie's temporarily postponed sitdown. The event drew closer with each successful snip of the no longer comforting legal red tape.

"He hasn't even tried," said Julie.

That was also true. She had been dating Terry for over three months and not once had he so much as hinted at the impending sitdown.

And, though she had let herself be blackmailed into Fowlers's preelection scheme, not for a moment did she believe the library-saving maneuver was actually going to work.

She had barely hung up on Fowler when the phone rang again.

"Got anything against corned beef and cabbage?"

"Don't tell me Steiner finally ran out of schnitzel."

Terry laughed, that so-male husky laugh for which Julie had such eager ears. "No, this is Feed-the-Starving-Brother Week. My sister invited us out to the boonies for supper tonight."

"I forgot you *had* a sister."

"She tries to forget it, too. Her kids think I'm the mailman."

Now it was Julie's turn to laugh. It occurred to her, then, that she had done a lot of laughing with Terry Brannigan. And no small amount of romantic daydreaming when she wasn't.

"I'll pick you up in ten minutes."

"Terry, that won't give me any time—"

"To change? My sister would love you if you came in a trash bag."

"Out to the boonies" turned out to be a trim green-and-white Cape Cod in one of the far western suburbs. Julie was surprised at the dark-haired young woman who greeted them at the door. She bore only a slight resemblance (was it the nose?) to the red-haired cop who claimed her as sister.

Peggy welcomed Julie as if she herself were a long-absent member of the family. Her warm hug was mild, though, compared to the explosive attack of her four children. Thundering down the stairs with a cry of "Uncle Terry!", they all but knocked him off his feet.

"It's only the uniform," smiled Peggy. "They do the same thing to the mailman."

At that, Terry gave his sister a gentle cuff on the chin and she obliged him with a feint to his trim middle. Julie smiled at the little affectionate boxing match, feeling for the first time in her life a loss at not having had any brothers—or a sister, for that matter.

In her series of apartment mates—five in the past three years—there had not been one single girl with whom Julie had wanted to get really close. The first had been a sullen moody lab technician who had a habit of reading in the bathroom.

She couldn't remember exactly why she or the other three girls had left. But the fifth had stormed out one evening, calling Julie a "prissy-pants Puritan" when she refused to let the girl's boyfriend stay the night.

"You must be something special," Peggy said to Julie when they were all seated around the table. "You're the very first girl he's brought around."

Terry's naturally healthy complexion grew even ruddier with an unprecedented blush.

"That's only because I've been paroled in his custody."

Peggy laughed, though Julie wasn't sure she knew anything about the library, or just how she and Terry had met.

"I'm surprised," said Peggy, passing the platter of corned beef, "that *any* girl would want to go out with him. He's never been known as a big spender."

Julie laughed, because there was a good deal of truth in his sister's remark. Sometimes all they ordered was coffee and apple strudel at the Blue Angel. Julie now wondered if it had been even that much for Terry while he had been waiting for the return of his hundred dollars.

"The name may be Irish," Peggy teased, "but when it comes to money, Terry's more the frugal Scot. Any day I expect him to show up in kilts."

Julie glanced over at Terry who was now busily cutting up corned beef for one of his small freckle-nosed nephews. She wondered if Terry Brannigan's children would all have freckles and red hair, too.

"I'd like to see that," she said aloud.

"Terry in kilts?" said Peggy. "You'd be disappointed. Bowlegged as a cowpoke."

But Julie knew Peggy's brother was anything but bowlegged. In fact, his body was as beautiful as his face. She had discovered that the first night she had gone to meet him at the policeman's warehouse gym and found him in a T-shirt and gym trunks.

He hadn't an ounce of excess fat, and his sturdy legs—solid and shapely in the calves—were as straight as his nightstick. A deliciously muscular five-foot-nine, Terry Brannigan looked like a title-ready middleweight at the peak of training.

The comparison wasn't that farfetched. Moreso,

because that was exactly how she had found him—dancing and dodging in the center of a makeshift boxing ring. With the little she knew about boxing, Julie still could see that Terry was out-maneuvering his gloved opponent, perhaps ten years younger, but certainly a good fifty pounds heavier. Hooting and whistling, at least ten other teen-age Latinos and blacks watched from outside the ring.

As the so grossly mismatched pair performed their rubber-soled ballet, Terry turned to give Julie a wink, and then his head rocked back on his shoulders as his young opponent landed a solid left on his jaw.

"Good boy." Terry acknowledged the boy's adroit timing with a gloved pat on the shoulder. Then he held up his right arm and aimed it toward the door. "Okay, you punks—all of you *scram*! *Vamos*!"

In the midst of boos and several taunts of "Chicken!", Terry climbed through the ropes, hopped down and planted a quick smack on Julie's lips. "Hi, Jewel."

Now and then he called her that. Julie wasn't ever sure whether it was merely a familiar adaptation of her name, or if he was telling her that he did, in fact, consider her something special.

Now he drew back at her wrinkled-up nose. "What is it—my deodorant has failed me?"

She shook her head. Not even the perspiration on his upper lip bothered her. Rather, she liked the saltiness of his kiss. To explain her reaction, she nodded toward his young overweight opponent, now tossing his gloves into the empty ring.

"Why boxing, Terry?"

"Why not?"

"It's so—barbaric."

"So are street fights, Julie." He reached for a towel draped over the ropes and began vigorously rubbing the back of his neck. "Better a cauliflower ear than a switchblade in the gut."

She thoughtfully digested that, turning again to look at the group of teen-age boys, now taking friendly pokes at each other as they went out the warehouse door. This was why Julie Chambers never saw Terry Brannigan on Tuesday or Thursday nights. And she was sure these biweekly boxing matches were not in the line of the policeman's paid-for-duty. She would never have known about his acts of Christian charity had she not come to the gym.

"How long have you been doing this, Terry?"

He shrugged. "I don't know—four, maybe five years. Why?"

"I just—think it's nice." And, on impulse, she went up on her toes and lightly kissed him on the same cheek that had taken the head-rocking left hook. Though she had allowed Terry any number of stolen kisses, it was the first time Julie had freely given him one herself.

"Has a temper like a tornado," Terry's sister went on, adding another to the dinner-table list of reasons why any girl shouldn't want to go out with him. Terry mutely sat through it all, as if his sister had long ago convinced him he was a poor candidate for sainthood.

"*Temper?*" said Julie doubtfully. Though they certainly had not always agreed when it came to the law and city politics, she never once had seen Terry Brannigan really lose his cool.

"You ever cross him up—you'll *know* it," said Peggy. "Half of that all-American blood is Italian."

Italian! So that explained his sister's dark hair and Terry's own dark brows. Yet, as she looked at him across the table, she wondered even more about something else. While neither the Irish nor the Italian half of his blood was famous for its peaceful tour through prime-of-life male arteries, he didn't behave anything like Bill Whittaker. With Bill, it had been a constant fight to keep his hands off her. Outside of a few brief kisses and holding hands out in Steiner's *Sommergarten,* Terry thus far had hardly touched her.

"And of course," said Peggy, "you already know he's not a big spender. But, then, any man saving up to buy a farm is apt to be a little tight with his money."

"Buy a *what*?" said Julie, almost choking on her mouthful of beef.

"A farm," said Peggy. "I thought you already knew that."

"No."

"Oops!" said Peggy. She glanced over at Terry. "Did I let a little secret out of the bag?"

"No," said Terry. "But, I *was* planning to show it to her first."

The rest of the visit was like wandering in a dream. Julie helped Peggy with the dishes, watched Terry romp in the front room with the kids, later helped him tuck them into bed. She said goodbye to his sister at the door. But it was all as if she weren't really there. And in her mind, she wasn't. She was back at the dinner table, screaming, *I don't believe it! I don't believe I'm hearing this!*

But driving back to the city with him, Julie knew

she *had* to hear it. "You're really serious?" she asked him. "About buying a farm?"

"Go ask my banker if I'm serious. I've stashed away practically every cent I've earned in the past five years." He reached up and adjusted the rear-view mirror. "Even got the place picked out. Should have it by the first of the year."

Julie slowly shook her head. She still didn't believe it—didn't *want* to believe it. "I thought you said you always wanted to be a policeman."

"Yeah, I know—but that was back when I was a kid. I'm not cut out for this blood-and-guts crime-stopper stuff." He nodded to his holster, between them on the seat. "I don't just go around pinching pretty protestors, Julie. I've seen some things that would straighten your hair."

He made a turn and they were on the ramp to the tollway.

"Some of the worst times are when it's one of those child-beating calls. Poor innocent little kid, face all bashed in, body full of bruises—" Even in the dimness of the car, Julie could see the deep shudder that went through him.

"But why a farmer, Terry? Why not a plumber or a bus driver or a TV repairman?"

"Because I'm sick to death of the city. That isn't living, Julie, it's surviving. I don't want my kids growing up thinking that's all there is to the world— that all God ever made were highrises, parking lots and garbage-dump alleys. I want them to know there are trees and grass and flowers and sunsets. . . ."

With his reasons for wanting a farm, Terry was telling her a good deal mre—that he loved his Creator's earthly works, and that he hoped to be

112

married and have kids. Unknowingly, he was also telling Julie Chambers he was not the man for her.

For some time Julie said nothing, fearful she might start crying.

But sometime during the long drive home, she also found herself thinking about something she had briefly wondered about earlier—the fact that there had been only seven around the table for corned beef and cabbage. There should have been eight.

"Where's Peggy's husband?"

"Where he's been the past three years." Terry nodded upward. "With the Good Lord."

"Oh. That's too bad." And those hungry, almost devouring hugs from his sister's children suddenly took on more meaning.

"Moved out to the suburbs because Peggy thought it would be safer. Got it with a Saturday Night Special—right out there in the sticks—when some punks held up the local bank."

He reached up and once again adjusted the rear-view mirror, as if to get a better focus on the sticks they were rapidly leaving behind.

"My sister had the bad luck to fall in love with a cop."

CHAPTER 10

WHY, LORD?

You must have known I would fall in love with him. And I could understand it if he was just a policeman. After all, this crazy mixed-up world needs them.

But, a cop who wants to be a farmer?

Such was Julie's prayer that Sunday in church—her same heartbroken cry, morning and night, each day for two solid weeks. The thought that ran through her, like a sharp knife, every time she saw him, every time he called.

But shouldn't she have known? Hadn't she feared, right from the start, that Terry Brannigan might break her heart?

The last Friday in August—payday for them both—Terry was in an especially magnanimous mood as they drove over to the Blue Angel, promising that this time they *would* order steak.

"Why break our record now?" she wanly smiled.

The doomed couple ate a hearty meal. Tonight, she finally had decided, was the end. Before the evening was over she was going to tell Terry she wasn't going to see him anymore.

But, when he pulled into the alley behind the Blue Angel, Julie wondered. Would she be able to sit across the table from Terry Brannigan and tell him something like that—to his face?

As it turned out, she didn't have to say anything directly to his face, because this time Terry didn't sit across from her, but right next to her at the lantern-lit table out in Steiner's *Sommergarten.*

"Be warmer this way," he said putting his arm across the back of her chair.

It was an unusually cool August night, and they were two of only a few brave souls out in the garden. Terry was in his policeman's uniform and black leather jacket and she, in a soft blue woolen skirt and white bulky-knit sweater.

"Or would you rather go inside?" he asked her, drawing her close.

"No. This is fine."

"Good. I hate whispering sweet nothings to you across a crowded room."

If she hadn't been so intent on her night's unhappy mission, Julie might have given him a little skeptical snort. So far, the cop's sweet nothings had been limited to "kumquat" and "gumdrop" and a few other items from that candy counter she was sure he had haunted as a child. Even now, with Steiner gone to fill their order and the other garden-sitting couples so wrapped up in themselves, Terry could easily have availed himself of a few items not on the menu. But, merely holding her hand now, he hadn't even tried to

115

sneak one of his usual stingy kisses. And wouldn't that make things easier for her tonight?

"How did it go last night?" she now asked him, referring to his usual Thursday night boxing sessions at the gym.

"I think maybe it's time we switched to aerobic dancing. Sugar Ray Fats nearly broke my nose again."

"Again?" She turned to him and, being so close, they all but rubbed noses.

"Yeah. Feel this." He took her hand and ran her index finger down his nose. Julie felt just the slightest bump at the lean bridge. "Football tryouts in high school."

"*Football?*"

Julie wrinkled her own nose, having about as much enthusiasm for that particular rib-crunching sport as she had for boxing. Besides, while he was excitingly muscular in a T-shirt and gym shorts, she just couldn't see Terry Brannigan in a football uniform.

"All I got out of that was a busted beak," he now said. "Didn't even make water boy."

"Poor baby." She gave him a sidelong glance. "It didn't spoil it, though. It's a beautiful nose."

Terry sat for a few moments, slowly rubbing his twice-battered nose. Possibly because it was still tender from the night before; more likely, because it was one of the rare times Julie Chambers had said something nice about him.

Careful, Julie warned herself. This wasn't the way to begin an evening that was supposed to be their last.

"Now this—" Terry said, borrowing her finger again and using it to tap his crooked tooth, "I earned when I was twelve, taking care of some fifteen-year-

116

old sex maniac who kept calling my sister dirty names."

It was hard to believe a twelve-year-old could "take care" of a fifteen-year-old. But then, hadn't his sister said something about his having a temper like a tornado?

"The other guy *lost* his teeth," he added. "*Two* of them."

Again Julie wondered what it would have been like to have a brother, especially one who might have been both able and willing to take care of all *her* name-callers.

"I wasn't too easy on the little girls, either, back in those days."

"I'll *bet* you weren't." She could well imagine the trail of broken hearts Terry Brannigan had left behind.

"Especially the two Shaughnessy sisters. Regular Grade-A Susie Snitchers." He raised his husky voice a few notches. "Terry did this. . .Terry did that. . ."

"And just what *did* sweet little innocent Terry do?" she asked, trying to keep a straight face.

"Well, speaking of the library—" he nodded in the direction of the old McDonough mansion. "Back then, of course, the old dump wasn't really anything because nobody'd lived in it for so long."

Julie had to remind herself that the cop had grown up in the very ghetto that was now his beat.

"Only some of the kids didn't believe it," he said. "That the old castle was really empty. To them it was the world's official haunted house."

Julie could well imagine that. Back in Kansas there had been an old abandoned farmhouse she and some other country kids had often visited in the hopes of being scared out of their wits. When she was twelve she had gotten more than she had hoped for—a furtive grab in the dark by hands not belonging to any ghost. The grabber received a surprise, too—a trip to the woodshed.

"Well, anyway," Terry went on with his tale-of-two-sisters, "this one morning before school—Halloween to be exact—I sneaked inside the old dump through one of the back windows. It was a perfect setup . . . a dark, spooky day. I waited for the two sisters to come by and, just when they got to the gate, I opened the front door and gave them my super deluxe Hound-of-the-Baskerville's howl."

Julie laughed.

"Yeah, I laughed, too. Until I got to school. I ended up standing in the corner."

Julie laughed again. What she really wanted to do, though, was give the cop one of those devouring kisses she so carefully held back from him—kisses she would never be able to give him.

"Now, if it had been *you*—" he said, giving her a little squeeze, "I wouldn't have minded standing in the corner. In fact, if I had been waiting for you—it wouldn't have been to *scare* you."

"Don't kid yourself," she told him, borrowing one of his own favorite expressions. "I was the *original* Suzie Snitcher back in Kansas."

"No kidding. *My girl?*"

"And skinny as a rail. Braces, too."

"Yeah? Well, you sure grew up nice." He gave her an appreciative glance. "What I can't figure out is those plowboys in Kansas—why they ever let you go."

"Simple," she said. But she did not tell Terry Brannigan about her own simple, yet successful "scare" tactics with the boys back home.

"I knew you were a rare gem that very first day," he said, again taking her hand. "Why do you think I sent you on that wild goose chase to City Hall?" He gave her the answer himself. "So I could cut you off at the pass on your way back."

He was, of course, talking about how he had met her on the way back from City Hall—the first time she had gotten into his parked car.

"I thought that was just an accident."

"Don't kid yourself. *Nothing* that happened after you came into the station that day was an *accident*." He tightened his arm around her. "You cost me a lot more than just a hundred bucks, Julie—"

She gave an unknowing look—rather difficult at such close range.

"—bribing all those other cops to swap duty with me, so I could be in the right place at the right time. City Hall isn't even on my beat."

Julie was silent a moment, recalling not only Terry's sudden appearance in a squad car the night of Operation Sidewalk, but his earlier timely appearance, on foot, the day of her children's parade.

"You mean—"

"That the pinch was phony?" He shook his head. "No, I'm not that sneaky, Julie. You were sure to be nabbed for that little caper—I just made sure I was the one who nabbed you. The only thing rigged was that courtroom scene."

Julie remembered feeling that the "trial" was somewhat strange—the seclusion of the judge's chamber; the absence of legal counsel—just the offender, the arresting officer, the court reporter—had caused even Bill Whittaker to think it fishy.

"You mean—"

"No," shaking his head. "That was all on the up-and-up, too. The only thing rigged about that was my arranging to have it all backstage—to save you embarrassment."

"And how were you able to do that?"

"By asking the judge for special handling." He gave her another little squeeze. "I told him you were my girl."

Something inside her sank at the way he said "my girl." She was sure, now, that their lantern-lit conversation tonight was no accident, either. The sweet nothings Terry had planned on whispering to her were really a series of true confessions.

"I would've moved in on you a lot sooner if it hadn't been for Prince Charming." Bill Whittaker, of course. "Lucky for him he bowed out when he did."

Julie fingered her water glass. There was no harm in letting Terry think Bill had bowed out rather than been booted out. She wondered what Terry would call it when he got the same treatment.

"Why are you telling me all of this, Terry?"

"Because I want everything straight with us, Julie. No more little secrets."

Julie turned her face away. Though she had vowed that tonight would be the night, she wasn't yet ready to be straight with Terry Brannigan.

"Julie?" he softly asked her. "Honey?"

When she didn't answer him, he reached over and gently turned her face back.

"You *are* my girl, *aren't* you?"

Julie closed her eyes. Partly because she was afraid she was going to cry; partly because she was sure he was now going to kiss her.

Mercifully, Steiner suddenly arrived with their schnitzel.

"You cops'll soon have to do your smooching somewhere else. Tomorrow the Blue Angel could be grounded."

Though it was hard to get her mind back on anything on earth, Julie was sure their host was referring to the cold weather just ahead and the closing of his *Sommergarten* until next summer.

"Don't listen to him," said Terry. "He's been saying that for the past two thousand years."

"Saying what?" said Julie.

"That he's selling out."

"Only this time I mean it," said Steiner. He sat down across from them at the table—a little courtesy he sometimes afforded his regular customers.

Steiner's property stretched out over five city lots. Two of them held the restaurant proper; the other three, the outdoor garden. The garden's winter closings were costing Steiner—taxes on the five lots were strangling him. He was hoping to sell the *Sommergarten* and then just operate the indoor restaurant.

"There's only one thing stopping me," he added.

"What's that?" said Terry, plunging his fork into his plateful of steaming noodles.

"The right price."

"How much?"

Steiner told him and both he and Julie raised their eyebrows at the figure.

"The city," said Steiner, "offered me considerably less."

"The *city*!" said Julie with her mouth full.

Steiner nodded. "Something about maybe using it for a library."

Julie almost choked on the noodles. "You're kidding."

Steiner reached over and punched Terry on the arm. "Tell your little *liebchen* that Steiner never kids about money."

"Steiner never kids about money," said Terry.

"How much less did the city offer you?" Julie asked, convinced now that Herman Steiner was serious.

"So much less," said Steiner, "that I laughed right in their faces."

When they came out of the Blue Angel, Terry found what appeared to be a religious tract under his windshield wiper. Claiming to be a means of spreading the "Good News," the pamphlet was nothing more than one so-called evangelist's bitter crusade against "organized religion."

"Boy, that really galls me," Terry said, tearing the tract into bits and tossing them into the alley. "The night before our Lord died, he prayed to the Father that someday we all would be one. Now you tell me, Julie—how the Father is going to answer the Son's prayer, if we all keep attacking each other."

Julie gave him no answer, and he apparently hadn't expected one, for he immediately went on.

"He's not going to work some kind of ecumenical miracle—force us into unity against our wills. *Thy kingdom come*—that's got to come from in *here*."

He tapped the badge which lay almost directly over his heart.

"That night in the garden—Gethsemane—He was a man, afraid of pain and death, just like the rest of us. But He was God, too. And He could see into the future, see how His own flock was going to be scattered, the terrible things we would say and do to each other, and do them like this guy—"

He nodded to the torn-up tract scattered in the alley.

"—in His very *name*. Those drops of blood in the garden—they were probably right from His heart. It wasn't the nails that killed Him, Julie—not even the lance. You know what I think He died of? A broken heart."

Terry had then sat back on the seat with a deep sigh, as if exhausted by his little off-the-cuff front-seat homily. And Julie wondered if he indeed hadn't missed his true calling, maybe belonged more in a pulpit than a squad car.

"Isn't it about time you asked me in?" Terry asked at her apartment door, "

"No. But it *is* time—"

"I told you before—I never molest girls when I'm in uniform."

He took the key from her and opened the door. Once inside, he tossed his leather jacket along with his holster and dark tie, onto a nearby chair.

"Nice place," he said, glancing about the front room. "But kind of big for just one, isn't it?"

"Yes," she admitted. "And I'll have to do something about that quite soon." She still had it in her purse—the notice from her landlord last week that her rent had been raised. "Either get a roommate or find a smaller place."

"Maybe you won't have to do either."

With that, he immediately embarked upon an uninvited, unguided tour of Julie's home. In the big dining room, he fingered the draperies, picked up a picture on the buffet, turned over an empty candy dish on the table—as if hot on the scent of a clue.

"You know—you're supposed to have a search warrant for this sort of thing," Julie told him from the bedroom doorway.

He even had the nerve to go right into her bedroom and begin manhandling the perfume, make-up, and other sundry girl-stuff scattered about the top of her vanity. Not did he miss her Bible on the nightstand beside her bed. He opened the book and let the blocks of pages flutter right to left, as if expecting some little secret to tumble out.

"What are you *looking* for?" she finally asked him.

"You. The real Julie Chambers behind that smart mouth." He came to her in the doorway and lifted her chin.

"Look who's talking."

"We make a good pair."

He reached for her waist, but she successfully eluded him. She didn't want to hear Terry Brannigan talk about pairs. Not with his arms around her, standing in her bedroom doorway.

When he followed her back into the front room, she asked him, "Why *did* you come up here?"

"I'm hungry."

"All you ate at Steiner's—how could you possibly still be hungry?"

"Steiner can't give me what I'm *really* hungry for."

The cop again reached for his prey, but again his wary target stepped out of range. "Here—" she now said, heading for the long coffee table in front of the couch. She picked up a stack of papers and thrust them out to Terry. "If you're so interested in the real me—read some of these."

The stack of papers was composed of the neatly typed and stapled versions of her "Tugboat Tommy"

124

stories—all eight of them. She really didn't expect him to read them. She had merely snatched at them in an attempt to sidetrack him, to give her time to rehearse her little speech: *It's really been fun, Terry, but tonight is the end.* If he ever got his arms around her, she knew she would be unable to deliver her little "swan song."

"Thanks," said Terry. "That's all I needed—some more paperwork." But he took the manuscripts from her.

"Terry, I've got to talk to you."

"Fine. I want to talk to you, too." He glanced at his watch. "But I have to run now—got the grave-yard shift."

"Tell you what, though," he said at the door. "I'll come by in the morning—for breakfast—and we can talk then."

"Good."

Leaning against the closed door, his parting kiss still warm on her mouth, Julie prayed. *Please, Lord, give me the right words in the morning . . . and the courage to say them. And please . . . don't let it hurt too much.*

But didn't it already hurt?

O, Lord, she later complained against her pillow, *if he has to be something else, why not a butcher or a banker? Or even a boxer?*

Why a farmer?

Julie suddenly awoke to the clatter of pots and pans in her kitchen—something she hadn't heard in over six months. Her brain cobwebby with sleep, she was at first frightened, then confused. Slowly last night began to come back to her.

Terry! How had he gotten in?

Quickly she snatched up her pink velour robe from the foot of the bed and headed for the bathroom. Julie hastily finger-combed a few stray locks from her forehead and then groaned at the bleary-eyed girl in the mirror. The only color in her face was the mark of a pillow-crease across her right cheek. Quickly she pulled on jeans and a sweater.

Oh, well. Ready or not, Terry Brannigan was going to see what he thought he wanted to see—the real Julie Chambers.

When she padded zombielike into the kitchen, she found him at the counter with an open carton of eggs, cracking one of them into a small bowl.

"Ah! Sleeping Beauty," he said over his shoulder. "Rapunzel—fresh from her tower."

"Very funny." She made a little face at him. "I know what I look like in the morning. And how did you get in here anyway?"

"Professional secret. I was a teen-age safecracker." His glance caressed her, as one might an abandoned kitten picked up in some alley. He himself looked especially alert, even after eight hours of patrolling. "How do you like your eggs—with or without shells?"

"Here. Let *me* do that."

He obligingly stepped aside and, with a spoon, Julie worked at scooping several ragged fragments of eggshell out of the bowl. Then she deftly cracked two more eggs and, with a fork, began beating them.

Terry sat on a nearby stool, softly whistling as she slowly melted the butter and poured the beaten eggs into the frying pan. He was whistling one—or maybe two—of the oldies written back when music was really music and not just a lot of noise. Julie wasn't sure which, though. Was it *Oh-You-Beautiful-Doll, You-Do-Something-to-Me*—or a crooked-toothed medley?

"Are you always so disgustingly cheerful in the morning?"

"Only when I'm having breakfast with a best-selling author."

"Oh, sure. Those manuscripts should bring in a big bundle—in a paper drive."

"Don't kid yourself." He shifted on the stool. "Those stories are little gems."

"You mean you actually *read* them?"

"Not last night, of course."

"This *morning?* "

"Bright and early. While Louisa May Alcott was still in there"—he nodded toward her bedroom— "sleeping like a log."

Julie kept her eyes on the skillet, diligently turning the curdled eggs. She entrusted her guest with only the simplest task—making the toast. This time there was no doubt as to which of the oldies he was whistling. And if she hadn't been so fearful of falling into her own tender trap, Julie might have smiled at the irony of it: The arresting officer's in a slightly off-key confession that he was a "Prisoner of Love."

Now, Julie prodded herself. *Tell him right now!*

No, she decided, going to the refrigerator for a jar of jam. *Not on an empty stomach.*

Terry stopped whistling only after they carried breakfast—the scrambled eggs, the toast, and coffee—out on trays to the coffee table in the front room. He made room for the two trays by moving her pile of manuscripts over to a nearby chair.

"I mean it, Jewel—those stories are really good."

"Well, thank you."

She had known the stories were good, the way any writer always knows, deep down, whether something is really good or not. Yet, because they were children's stories—not an adult novel or short story— she considered them on the bottom rung of literary achievement. She could almost hear her father's similar assessment: *This is what you went to college for—to write kid stuff?*

At the same time, Terry Brannigan's unsolicited critique of her "Tugboat Tommy" pleased her. And not for the first time did it occur to Julie the importance she had begun to attach to what Terry Brannigan might happen to think about this or that. The only thing on which they seemed to have any real disagreement was the library.

And the farm, of course.

As they sat down beside each other on the couch Julie decided that right now she was going to tell him. Breakfast or no breakfast, she would have to set this beautiful farm-happy cop straight—right now.

She drew in a tremulous breath. "Terry—"

"You know, you ought to try to get those things published." He reached for a piece of toast, nodding his head toward her pile of manuscripts on the chair.

Julie had never thought of that. Her motive in writing the stories had been merely to entertain her small listeners at the library and at the same time teach them language, as well as some simple but vital Christian truths. If she hadn't done the latter—given the stories Christian emphasis—it all *would* have been a complete waste of time.

"I like the way you worked in all the "Blesseds"—

128

a different one in each story. The whole Sermon on the Mount, without being the least bit preachy.''

He took a bite of the toast.

"I'm sure *that* was no accident, Julie—a really neat piece of writing.''

Indeed it had been no accident, Julie had been fully aware of what she was doing. But she had thought it would take a preacher—or at least a student of the Bible—to detect her riverboat version of the Master's teaching.

"But you left out one very important 'Blessed',''' he now said, setting his unfinished piece of toast back on the plate.

Julie glanced at him, wondering if what he said was true. No, she was sure she had covered all of the Beatitudes in her "Tugboat Tommy" stories. She didn't know Terry meant one of his own.

"Blessed are ye who suffer the name of 'pig' in the performance of duty—"

He wiped his fingers with one of the paper napkins, also on the tray.

"—for one day ye shall inherit a treasure.''

Because he was giving her that kitten-caressing look again, Julie turned her face away. But he reached over and gently turned it back. "Sweetheart?''

It was the same heart-melting tone he had used the night before when he had called her "Honey.'' And Julie's answer was the same as the night before— simply closing her eyes.

Suddenly she was in his arms.

"I *need* you, Julie!''

"Oh, Terry—"

And then, nothing mattered but his arms. And his mouth. And her wish that his kiss would never end.

CHAPTER 11

HER PARENTS MET HER at the airport in Tampa. Julie could see in her mother's face all the questions she would surely ask about the suddenness of their daughter's long-promised visit.

Julie already had a pat answer: The Midtown Branch Library had finally closed. She only hoped her mother wouldn't suspect there might be another reason why she suddenly needed to get away.

That very day, Monday morning, the city truck had showed up at the library. It was twice the size of the one she and Paddy Fowler's boys had used the night of Operation Sidewalk. The workmen were also almost twice the size of Bill Whittaker and his classmates. They had been in no great rush, though, to get the cartons of books loaded onto the truck. And Julie had spent several agonizing hours behind her empty desk, afraid that the still-connected telephone might ring, and it would be Terry. Or Paddy Fowler.

She had cleared her travel plans only with the city,

informing them that she was taking her long-post-poned and much-needed vacation.

Only when the big jet lifted off the runway at O'Hare, did Julie let out a quivering sigh of strangely heartsick relief. As she looked down at the diminishing Chicago shoreline, she knew she was leaving a good part of herself behind.

The Sunshine State gave the fugitive from the Prairie State a hot and humid welcome. As she and her parents walked out of the air-conditioned Tampa airport and into the parking lot, Julie—coming from a city cooled by soft September breezes—felt as if someone had just slapped her in the face with a steaming-wet towel.

In her father's small air-conditioned Toyota, they traveled the twenty or so miles to St. Petersburg; seven of them, over a single bridge spanning the bay between Tampa and the city to the south which the retired Kansas couple now called home.

Julie momentarily denied the ache in her heart, "oohing and aahing" over the lush bloom-laden shrubbery and feathery palms—the state's unique flora growing in profusion at the side of the road. She would later learn of Florida's equally unique fauna.

Once she was settled into her parents' spare bedroom, and all the customary small talk was over, Julie found herself waiting for the third degree from her mother—not only about the suddenness of her visit, but also the inevitable question of when she was going to settle down and get married.

But, if anyone seemed finally settled, it was her parents. Having grown up with them on the farm where everything went according to the clock, Julie was continually amazed at the leisurely pace of her parents' adopted Florida lifestyle. On the farm, they had been up before the chickens. In the condominium it didn't matter when, or even if, they got up.

Breakfast was a casual affair, often served out on the small poolside balcony—whenever the stomach, not the clock, signaled. Lingering over coffee, savoring not only the warm nutty brew but the damp fragrance of the morning, made one thankful to be alive. Afterward, with the dishes in the automatic washer, there were hours spent basking in the sun, on one of the many lawn chairs surrounding the sprawling retirement community's large amoeba-shaped swimming pool. Julie's mother might sit and lazily knit. Julie's father—and this was another source of amazement—might carelessly browse through the morning's newspaper.

Julie herself merely lay on one of the lounges, soaking in the delicious poolside warmth, and letting all the fumes and frenzy of life in the big city gently ooze out of her pores.

That very first morning, glancing over at Paula Chambers, knitting beside her on one of the lawn chairs, Julie marveled at her mother's brown and slender bare legs. She had never before seen her mother's legs—not that much of them. And certainly never bare.

As for her father, he didn't look the least like a retired farmer—or a man who had had a heart attack. While he had always appeared robust and windchafed back on the farm, Peter Chambers, tanned and leathery in a blue polo shirt and white slacks, now looked like a captain on an ocean liner.

There were other little Florida surprises in store for

Julie the first full day—the little green or black chameleons that crept out of the foliage and down to the pool to try out some new colors at the water's edge; those little red-and-black "lovebugs"—always in pairs—performing aerial stunts over the lawn chairs as if indeed they had been permanently mated.

Each night a small nocturnal hopscotch parade of toads and frogs made its way into the pool with any after-sundown Winston Park swimmers. Some of the frogs were the size of Julie's fist. She was sure they, like the capricious chameleons, made their homes in the lush greenery just beyond the cement apron of the pool.

"Not all of them," said her mother. "Some of them hide out in there." And she nodded toward one of the big folded umbrellas on a nearby poolside table.

Yes, Julie Chambers had guts. But in the entire two weeks she spent in Florida, not once did she ever open one of those umbrellas.

In the middle of that first day, while her mother was up in her air-cooled kitchen preparing lunch and her father was shopping for cream soda to go along with their sandwiches, Julie lay in one of the lounge chairs, looking up at the clouds. Suddenly those clouds turned black and began rolling in, stirring up a sudden breeze that sent the Winston Park palms waving their feathery fronds as if in frantic warning.

Because it all came so suddenly, Julie quickly ran indoors to sound a duck-and-cover alarm as she had numerous times back in a Chicago tornado alert. Here, on the East Coast, she was sure it would be called something else.

But her mother merely slapped another glob of mayonnaise onto a slice of bread. "Oh, this happens

133

often about this time of day." She didn't even bother closing the glass balcony doors at the sudden downpour of rain. "It'll all be over in ten minutes."

And she was right. When Julie's father returned, they sat out on that very balcony with their sandwiches and soda, the pool below shimmering in the once-again bright and hot Florida sun.

In addition to the cream soda, Peter Chambers had also come back with a copy of the *Kansas City Star*—the very paper he had refused to read back on the farm. Later, while the three of them were again lounging down at the pool, Julie's father broke into her quiet little reverie.

"Say, Julie, here's an item you'll probably be interested in." He handed the paper across to her and pointed with a sun-browned finger to a small article somewhere on a back page. "Probably picked this up from the Chicago paper."

Julie took off her sunglasses and read:

CITY AT ODDS OVER "LANDMARK"

CHICAGO—City councilmen yesterday found themselves locking horns with the Chicago Landmark Commission over the old McDonough mansion slated for imminent destruction to make way for construction of the new expressway.

The building was willed to the city 15 years ago by the lone heir of Kevin McDonough, an Irish immigrant who became one of the Midwest's first millionaires. The mansion has since housed a branch library in what is now known as the Midtown Ghetto—a rapidly deteriorating community of Hispanics and blacks.

At the recent request of the head librarian, the Landmark Commission had been studying the possibility of declar-

134

ing and preserving the old mansion as a Chicago land-mark. Their investigations, they claim, have turned up some evidence that the building may have been designed by the world-famous architect Louis Henri Sullivan, one of the forerunners of modern city architecture.

The initials "LHS" chiseled into the cornerstone of the red-brick mansion, however, are the commission's only clue and not sufficient evidence to deter the city's engineers from razing the old building to make way for an expressway entrance ramp.

Most vocal in the last-ditch effort to preserve the McDonough Mansion has been one of the city fathers, Alderman P. J. (Paddy) Fowler who has described his fellow councilmen as "a bunch of bums who wouldn't know a landmark from a landmine."

Fowler has promised to continue what he terms a "fight to the finish." But, with the city wrecking crew only a block away, it appears to be only a matter of days before the dubious landmark is demolished.

"Isn't that the place where you work, Julie?" asked her father when she handed the newspaper back to him.

"*Used* to," she said bitterly. She was fuming over two particular phrases in the news story: "last-ditch effort" and "recent request of the head librarian." If Ellen Gray's five-year-old letters were last-ditch or recent, things must have changed a great deal in the world of English and journalism since Julie Chambers had studied both.

"What will you do, dear," asked her mother, glancing up from her needlework, "now that you've lost your job."

"Probably look for another one." Actually, she hadn't thought that far ahead.

"At another library?"

"No. That job was just an accident."

"I thought you were writing a book," said her father.

"Well, I did do some writing—" But she did not say any more, still reluctant to admit that all she had written in three years were eight children's stories and twelve puppet plays.

"Why can't you move down here and live with us?" said her mother. "We have the extra bedroom— and you'd be away from that awful Chicago weather."

Yes, thought Julie, *and I'd be away from something—someone—else.* "Don't tempt me," she said aloud.

"Unless there's someone really special back there," her mother said hopefully.

Special? Oh, he was special all right. It was because he was just that—so terribly special—that she was here.

"You never mention any young men," said her mother, setting aside her needlework. "Don't you ever date?"

"Of course—I go out once in a while."

"Well, I'm glad to hear that."

"So am I," said her father. "I'd hate to think you were turning into one of those freaky women's libbers."

"Oh, Peter!" said her mother, as if such a notion were ridiculous.

"Well, she was always pretty snippy with the boys."

"Only farmboys," said her mother. "She hated anything connected with the farm."

"Since when?" said her father.

"Since always," said her mother.

When Julie didn't dispute this, her father looked over at her and demanded, "Why? What's wrong with the farm?"

"Nothing," said Julie. "For *some* people."

"But not you?"

"You know Julie always craved adventure," said her mother. "How much action was there down on the farm?"

Was that the real reason she had left Kansas for Chicago—merely to search for adventure? Had all those lofty ideas about changing the wicked world with her writing merely been a convenient smoke screen? And all those deprived Latinos and blacks— were they merely supporting players in the Great Escape? *O Lord, I hope not*. That would make her as phony as Paddy Fowler in his election-time concern for saving the library.

Because such thoughts made her uncomfortable, Julie got up from her lawn chair and adjusted the strap on her swimsuit.

"I'll bet there are a lot of city slickers who'd give their right arms to be out in the country—out on a farm," said her father.

"You're probably right," said Julie. She was thinking not only of the kids at the library, but one other city slicker she knew.

"Well, nobody's trying to keep you down on the farm now, Julie," said her mother. "I'm talking about Winston Park. There should be enough excitement for you here."

"Oh, sure," said her father, "watching all us golden-agers sky-diving."

The rest of that week was spent in seeing the sights—for Julie's benefit, of course—at the same slow-moving Florida pace. Julie was glad Disneyworld was not included in the tour. She was more interested in the numerous sunken gardens and in visiting Venice—so like its channel-wound namesake across the sea.

And the ocean!

The first weekend they drove clear across the peninsula to Cocoa Beach where, on Sunday, Julie stood entranced at the edge of the vast, seemingly endless sea. And, like the surge of the rolling waves, she could feel emotion swelling within her, echoing the hymn she and her parents had sung earlier, along with the rest of the transient congregation, at a small roadside chapel on their way to the coast.

O yes, Lord—how great Thou art!

Early the following week they drove the two miles from Winston Park to The Pier, a four-story upside-down triangular building at the end of a long cement pier jutting out into the Tampa Bay. There, after browsing in the several irresistible gift shops, the three of them had an enormous seafood lunch topped off by a gigantic wedge of key lime pie—a must for every tourist's palate.

They lazily strolled back down the big pier, watching the people fishing off either side, occasionally stopping so Julie could get a close-up, through one of the handy telescopes, at the boats out in the bay, or of the seagulls gracefully dipping and diving overhead. She squealed in delight when a dolphin arced out of the water and into the air, as if to draw attention from the poaching pelicans along the guardrails, waiting for a handout from one of the fisherman's poles.

138

The even slower and more casual stroll back down the pier told Julie the sightseeing tour was coming to an end. She would, she feared, now spend the rest of her vacation in the quiet confines of Winston Park, soaking in more of the Florida sun—and fielding more of her parents' poolside questions about Julie Chambers' future.

Thursday, the day before her flight back to Chicago, Julie's parents took a bus trip to Busch Gardens with a group of other Winston Parkers. Since they had planned the trip long before Julie decided to drop from the sky into their little slow-motion world, she insisted that they go.

Being left to her own devices suited her just fine. By now, she was anxious to get off somewhere on her own where she wouldn't have to answer any more painful questions. She needed to collect her thoughts—wasn't that why she had come?—and indeed do some serious thinking about her future.

In a loose-flowing sleeveless cotton print dress, and wearing her new Florida sandals, Julie got behind the wheel of her father's Toyota. With an overstuffed floral denim beachbag and one of her mother's blankets beside her on the seat, she drove the sixteen or so miles from Winston Park to the Gulf of Mexico.

As she drew nearer the Gulf, Julie began to wonder if maybe she *should* pack up and move in with her parents. Surely she would be able to find some kind of work in St. Petersburg. If not, maybe her parents would allow her the privilege of being a writer in residence, and she could begin that serious novel she often thought she had in her. Wouldn't a best-seller justify all that money they had spent on her education?

If she made the move soon enough, packing the minute she got back to Chicago, she could forget all about Paddy Fowler and his last-ditch effort to save the library.

And she wouldn't have to deal with that other so-much-more-painful matter.

Reaching the Gulf, Julie soon found herself enthralled by the elegant, ostrich-legged beachhouses along the sandy shore. She easily found a parking space near one of the beaches, a small miracle back on Chicago's lakefront.

Beachbag in hand, blanket over her other arm, Julie struck out over the white sand to set up her temporary camp on the still-deserted beach. She soon had her sandals off and was padding barefoot along the water's edge. Feeling something hard beneath one of her toes, she bent down and picked up a tiny rainbow-tinted seashell. She picked up another and, moments later, another. There must have been thousands strewn about the beach, and Julie soon found her pulled-up print skirt loaded with the tiny shells.

She was aware of the cry of seagulls overhead, almost as if they were laughing at her childlike behavior. But, with each unique addition to her collection, Julie could only marvel at the boundless imagination of the Creator of such an endless variety of seashells.

Clutching her treasure-laden skirt, Julie waded knee-high into the warm waters of the gulf, lifting her head to look at the clouds. They, too, were always different. And these seemed even whiter and fluffier than any she had ever seen back in Chicago, and somehow closer—as if she had only to reach upward and touch one.

Again awed by the majesty of His creation, she now closed her eyes in silent communion with her Lord. And with the warm water lapping at her bare legs, she stood entranced, totally unaware of the passage of time.

Finally with a deep sigh she opened her eyes. Amazingly those same white, fluffy clouds she had thought she could touch had suddenly turned black and were ominously churning about in the heavens. The breeze, too, had begun whipping her dark hair back from her face, and the soft slap of warm water against her knees had become ever-swelling waves.

She didn't realize she was witnessing the birth of another sudden Florida squall—not until the rain hit her upturned face.

"Oh!" With a sudden start, Julie let go of her skirt, spilling her freely gathered hoard of seashells back into the sea from whence they had come.

Then, as if scornfully rejecting her involuntary offering, a sudden massive rolling wave thrust most of the shells back, engulfing Julie, sending her sprawling on the wet sand. She scrambled to her bare feet and began running for cover—as if she weren't already totally drenched. Just as foolish was the fact that there *was* no cover on the open stretch of sand.

"Up here!" She heard a sharp feminine command.

Julie squinted up through the pelting raindrops to see a woman in the open doorway of one of the stilt-legged houses. With a brisk beckoning motion of her hand, she urged Julie to come up.

The farm girl who had often climbed into her father's hayloft scrambled easily up the ladder to the beachhouse. She breathed a quivering sigh of relief after the door had been quickly slammed shut.

"Thanks!" She swiped at the water on her face. "You'd think by now I'd be used to it."

The woman was laughing. And if Julie hadn't been so preoccupied with the little puddle she was making on the expensive-looking carpet, she might have noticed that there something familiar about her rescuer.

"It takes more than a few days' vacation to get used to the whims of La Femme Florida."

"Julie raised her dripping head. "How did you—"

"Know you weren't a native? I was watching you, down on the beach. You can always tell us tourists— we're the ones with the bent-over shell-hunting backs."

It was Julie's turn to laugh now. But when the woman handed her a large beach towel, her expression grew serious. "Don't I *know* you?" she asked the tall slender woman standing before her in a halter and shorts.

In answer to her question, the woman bent down and peered into Julie's wet face. "Julie? Julie Chambers?"

"Ellen Gray! I don't *believe* it!"

And then the two of them were in a soggy embrace—like two long-separated sisters.

"Only it's not Gray anymore," said Ellen. "It's Jackson."

"*Married?*" Julie immediately was sorry for the raw disbelief in her question, but Ellen Jackson good-naturedly waved it aside.

"I know it *is* hard to believe—that any man would want to marry me. I *was* an insufferable, stuffy old maid."

Julie opened her mouth as if to politely disagree, but her hostess also waved that aside.

142

"And don't try to tell me I wasn't. I was a lot of stupid things back then. But that was before Leonard came along and changed my whole life. Led me not only to the altar, but to the Lord, as well."

Julie's mouth dropped open again, this time in surprise—and awe. That was why she had not immediately recognized the former Midtown librarian. It wasn't the halter and shorts—or even the deep Florida tan. It was love of the Lord glowing in her smooth bronzed face.

"I'll tell you all about it," said Ellen. "After I get you out of those wet clothes."

Moments later Julie, wrapped in a white terry cloth robe, sat sipping hot coffee from a gigantic mug. Ellen Jackson sat facing her, at a small table by a large picture window overlooking the bay.

"There'll be some doughnuts to go along with this," said Ellen over her own heavy mug, "as soon as Leonard gets back."

"So *tell* me," urged Julie, like a romantic school girl, more interested in a good love story than any doughnuts.

"Well," said Ellen, setting her mug down, "we met in New York at a bookseller's convention—I, as a browsing children's librarian; Leonard, a somewhat disenchanted editor working at one of those big secular publishing houses. We started talking, and before long we found we had something in common— we were both sick of the junk being passed off as children's books."

Julie took another small sip of the steaming coffee. If she had been a real librarian, she would have been aware of what was going on in the publishing world. But she hadn't even bothered to open the publishers' catalogs or read the book reviews—not since the library board had stopped authorizing any new purchases for the Midtown Branch Library.

"We also found that each of us—never having been married—had a little private nest egg stashed away. And, as we kept bumping into each other at various convention workshops, one thing led to another and before the thing was over, we were talking about a partnership, starting our own publishing house."

Julie's storytelling coffee mate now smiled.

"We had no idea, then, just how intimate that partnership was going to become."

Ellen Jackson picked up the coffeepot and refilled Julie's cup. When Julie reached for the sugar, she noticed Ellen's glance at her own ringless left hand.

"I'm surprised *you're* not married by now—that some young Chicago bull hasn't corralled you."

Julie shook her head.

"That's okay," Ellen nodded. "Marriage is too serious a matter to rush into." She smiled a bit ruefully. "It took me almost forty years to find the right man."

"So, go on with your story," Julie prodded, eager to take the focus off herself.

"Well, before too long, I left my cushy little job back in Fantasyland and plunged right back into the asphalt jungle, New York style. By then, Leonard not only had rented a small office on Madison Avenue, but he also had a typist and a printer lined up. Had a name for our new little company, too."

Ellen dreamily refilled her own coffee cup and sat the pot back down on its trivet, as if herself enthralled by her own story.

"He was determined that, as Christian publishers, we should be at least a small light in the darkness—"

Better to light one candle . . . Julie thought, again recalling her own noble—but now defunct—ambitions when she had first landed in Chicago.

"—publish only the best children's books with a truly Christian flavor. We do just that now, and we call ourselves the Lamplighter Press."

"Oh, I *like* that," said Julie.

"And in case you're wondering just what we're doing out here on the Gulf like beachcombers, instead of slaving back at the office—"

Julie shook her head. She suspected a lot of New Yorkers came down out of their asphalt jungle to refuel in the Florida sunshine.

"We drive down every three or four months and rent one of these outrageous treehouses. And we *do* indulge in a good deal of combing—" Ellen nodded over to several cardboard cartons standing in a corner of the room, bathed in a warm splash of sunlight now streaming through the big window "—reading through three tons of unsolicited manuscripts in the hope of finding maybe just a single good one."

Her eyes still on the cardboard cartons, Julie suddenly thought of some other manuscripts. She wasn't quite sure why she had bothered to bring the stories with her to Florida—and more specifically to the beach that morning—unless it was to try to convince herself that her "Tugboat Tommy" stories were good and ought to be sent to some publisher, as *someone back in Chicago* had suggested.

"Well, it could be worse," she told Ellen Jackson. "At least all those stories are still *dry*."

"What do you mean?" said Ellen.

Julie nodded toward the beach. "My own ton of soggy manuscripts—left out in the rain."

They both scrambled down the wooden ladder—Ellen Jackson ahead of Julie. She also reached it first—Julie's denim beachbag which had fallen over on its side in the sudden morning squall.

"Thank God," she said, pulling out the big beach towel which Julie had—only as an afterthought—stuffed into the top of the bag.

Julie wasn't sure what all the fuss was about—after all, they were just some silly children's stories.

Once Ellen had found the manuscripts—all eight of them—the two women then sat down on the already dry blanket Julie had earlier spread out on the sand. It was amazing how—less that twenty minutes after the storm—it seemed as if it hadn't even rained.

"I knew it—I just *knew* it!" Ellen cried sometime later, shaking her still honey-colored head for perhaps the seventh or eighth time. "These stories are fantastic!"

Hugging her terry-clothed knees, Julie knew she should be feeling good about that. But she was again thinking of someone else who had called the "Tugboat Tommy" stories "little gems."

"And that policeman—he's *darling*!"

Julie's heart skipped a beat. She looked over at Ellen in amazement. How could Ellen Jackson possibly know anything about *him*?

"I'm surprised you didn't bring him into the stories sooner. But, no, maybe it's just as well—he nearly steals that last story right out from under little Tommy."

Ellen thumbed back a few pages in the last manuscript, as if for another look at the policeman she thought "darling."

"Too bad he's only on paper. The world could use

146

more men like him. How did you ever dream *him* up, Julie?''

Julie turned her face toward the gulf, hoping Ellen wouldn't see in her eyes what was going on inside her breast. She hadn't been aware that she had allowed a certain fictitious policeman to almost steal the story from her little riverboat hero. She wished, now, that she *had* merely dreamed up a certain red-haired cop who, in real life, had stolen a good deal more than just a story.

She wished, too, that she hadn't let a few passionate kisses send her running home to Mama like a frightened school girl. She should have stayed in Chicago and settled the matter once and for all.

"You know what you've done?" asked Ellen Jackson.

Julie sadly nodded. *Merely postponed the agony.*

"Given Lamplighter Press a whole new series."

Ellen hugged Julie's manuscripts to her breast as if they might be some priceless treasure she had found down on the beach.

"We could call them Lighthouse Books," she said, looking out to the Gulf as if the future were unfolding before her like some slowly approaching ship. "Yes, that would be perfect. It would tie in not only with our overall lamplighter theme—but with the stories themselves. You know, the lighthouse little Tommy always keeps watch for . . . as well as their Christian message—Christ's being the Light of the World. . . ."

"Yes," Julie nodded, finally catching some of her companion's excitement about the new series. Or maybe it was the knowledge that Julie Chambers had, after all, done something worthwhile.

"God is so *good*!" said Ellen, still hugging the stories close and looking up at the now cloudless sky. "I'm sure it's no accident, Julie—your coming to this beach today."

Julie thoughtfully looked at the editor sitting beside her on the blanket. How many times had she herself said something about God working in mysterious ways. *Was* that why she suddenly had come to Florida—not merely to run from heartache—but to "light up" the lives of some children with eight little books?

Lord, couldn't You have done it some easier, more gentle way?

"What would you think of coming to New York?" Ellen broke into her thoughts.

Julie stared back at her, her dark eyes opening wide.

"We need a good editor. That would free Leonard and me to go out and build up our sales force. And that's vital," said Ellen. "No matter how good the books, they're no good to anybody if we don't sell them."

Julie opened her mouth, but nothing came out. The very thought staggered her. Here—out on a beach blanket—her dream, bigger than she had dared to imagine, was coming true. She had hoped to invade the media at the very bottom rung of the ladder and perhaps—with the right phrase here, a different approach there—make a tiny stab at piercing the pagan darkness. Now, she was being offered a job right at the top. And in New York!

A few years ago, she would have leaped at such an offer. Now it gave her a speech-stopping lump in her throat. Could she do that—actually pack up and forever leave Chicago? Leave the Midtown ghetto and all those beautiful people who had worked their way into her heart? Leave *him* behind?

Lord, is that the answer? Could God be handing it to her like a bow-tied Christmas package—an easy way out? What better way to end a hopeless romance than to pack up and leave for good!

Still, Julie found herself hesitating. "I don't know, Ellen."

"You'd have plenty of time to write," the editor coaxed. "We certainly wouldn't stifle our very best author."

"I'd really have to think about it."

"You do that." Ellen patted the pile of manuscripts. "Either way—New York or Chicago—you've got a contract for *these* books."

CHAPTER 12

NEW YORK OR CHICAGO. The names of the two cities kept crowding Julie's mind as Flight 994 carried her through turbulent Friday night skies back to the Windy City.

She felt somewhat remiss at not having shared her new author's status with her parents before getting on the plane. But she wanted the decision—New York or Chicago—to be totally hers.

Leonard Jackson, finally returning to the beach-house with his box of breakfast doughnuts, had been as enthusiastic as his wife in his appraisal of the "Tugboat Tommy" stories. He had informed their new author that her contract for the series of Light-house Books would carry a clause claiming any future literary works by Julie Chambers for Lamplighter Press before any other publisher got a crack at them. As for Julie's coming to New York to work as an editor, he had no question about that, either. But he, like Ellen, understood that Julie needed time to think about it.

It certainly was a more tempting offer than the one made by the Chicago Public Library board. Sitting behind a desk on New York's Madison Avenue sounded more glamorous than struggling with the wheel of some broken-down bookmobile—or spending the rest of her life back on a farm.

As the plane pulled out of another air pocket, Julie found herself recalling the night she had gotten her last college creative writing award. Her English professor, Dr. Wainwright, had singled her out at the little punch-and-cookies reception afterward.

"You're an excellent writer, Miss Chambers," he told her, "one of the few original thinkers on campus. You could even become an *important* writer."

"Well, thank you."

"But, you'll never do it stuck out on a farm. You need to break away—broaden your horizons, get into the swim of life. Otherwise you'll have nothing more important to say than whether it's going to rain on the wheat, or the price of hogs is going up."

That bit of timely advice had been all Julie had needed then to make up her mind about leaving the farm. And Leonard Jackson's parting shot yesterday—all but echoing his wife's—kept coming back to her now as she fastened her seatbelt for the jet's descent through the clouds over Lake Michigan and its final landing at O'Hare.

"There is no such thing as a coincidence, Julie—not if we believe God truly works in our lives. I can't believe your coming here today was an accident—any more than Ellen's and my meeting at a booksellers' convention was an accident."

By the time the plane landed, Julie had made up her mind to take the job in New York, and forget about any and all who might have a claim on her heart in Chicago.

Still, when she got to her apartment door, she momentarily panicked at the sound of her phone's persistent ring. Finally, she snatched it up after its fifth, or maybe twenty-fifth, ring.

"Lucky for you it's been raining all week," said Paddy Fowler.

Julie immediately knew what the alderman meant. A full week of September rain had again halted work on the city's new expressway, and only because of that had Julie Chambers not missed her reluctant rendezvous with the wrecking crew.

"Monday for sure," said Fowler. "I checked the three-day forecast and there's not even a hint of rain."

Apparently it was no accident, either, that Julie had not missed the sitdown, after all. Wouldn't that send her off to New York with a clearer conscience, knowing she had truly done her utmost to save the Midtown Library?

She barely had replaced the receiver when the phone rang again. This time it was Bill Whittaker. He sounded as if he didn't know that Julie had been away two whole weeks—or that it had been longer since they had dated. After all, he did have something important he wanted to tell her. Just that very morning he had finally learned he had passed his bar exams.

"How about helping me celebrate?"

"All *I* want to do is crawl into bed," she told him, not only tired but still a little airsick.

"Tsk, tsk!" said Bill. "Is that what they taught you in the land of sunshine?"

She answered him with a loud yawn. She was too tired to be bothered by his doube entendre or to even ask him how he knew she had been in Florida. With the receiver caught between her ear and her shoulder, Julie reached down to take off her first shoe. She was dying to peel off her clothes, take a hot shower, and get into her own familiar bed.

"And anyway," said Bill, "I wasn't talking about tonight. I meant Sunday—going to one of my classmate's wakes."

"A *wake*? You call that a *celebration*?"

"That's what we always call it when one of the guys gets hitched. Fanelli's taking the plunge Sunday—I thought maybe you'd like to go with me."

"I don't know, Bill—" She took off the other shoe. "I'm too tired now to think. Call me tomorrow."

Julie awoke in the morning with a start, thinking her alarm had gone off. No, this was Saturday. Besides, she no longer had any job to get up for. Then she realized it was the telephone that had awakened her— and it was still ringing. Sleepily, she reached toward the nightstand. "Hello?" she yawned into the receiver.

"*Julie!*" There was raw relief in Terry Brannigan's voice. "Where have you *been*?"

"Away," she said simply, with anything but relief in her voice. *O Lord—why did you let him call?*

"I've been out of my mind," said Terry. It was probably the first time his hitherto reliable grapevine had not yielded him a satisfying crop of information. "Calling everywhere—"

Everywhere but the office of his friendly neighborhood alderman, Julie thought wryly.

"Not even a postcard," he said accusingly.

"I didn't have your address," she said truthfully. She couldn't even recall what street his rooming house was on.

"In care of the police station—that would have been enough, Julie."

She winced at the obvious hurt in his voice. "I was terribly busy, Terry."

"So busy you couldn't pick up the phone and tell me you were going away?"

She didn't answer him. How could she tell him he was the very reason she had gone away—the real reason she would soon be going away permanently.

"I hope you aren't all booked up tomorrow," he finally said.

"I'm *always* booked up for Sunday," she reminded him. There was the nine o'clock worship service and then Bible study afterward down in the basement of the North Shore Church.

"I mean later," said Terry. "I'm standing up for my cousin's wedding."

"It must be contagious," she said, recalling Bill Whittaker's earlier invitation.

"I'd like to take you to the reception," he said. "That is, if you think you could stand me in a tuxedo."

She tried not to think of that: Terry Brannigan in a tuxedo!

"I can't, Terry. I've got to get up at the crack of dawn the next morning." She was grateful to have so handy an excuse.

And though his missing-persons grapevine apparently had failed him once; if Julie thought he didn't know what the next morning was, she was badly mistaken.

"You mean you're actually going to go through with that harebrained sitdown scheme of Fowler's?"

"Of course I am."

"I thought—"

"Well, you thought wrong."

During the long silence following, Julie could almost hear his putting the pieces together—her two-week trip without any notice, the coldness in her voice now that she was back—wondering if he were getting a none-too-polite brushoff.

Julie decided to quickly end his confusion. "I've got a lot of things to do this morning, Terry—got to start packing. I'll be moving to New York next weekend."

Again there was silence on the other end of the wire—the deadly aftermath of her own little early-morning atomic bomb.

"I'm coming right over, Julie!"

"I won't open the door," she warned him, panic rising in her breast.

"Then I'll *kick* it in!"

He didn't have to kick in the door of her apartment. By the time he exploded out of the elevator, Julie had the door open and was waiting for him.

In the half-hour it had taken him to get from his home to hers, Julie had had time to get dressed, slipping into an old frayed flannel shirt and a pair of faded jeans from her days back on the farm. She also purposely did not put on any make-up and had left her hair up in rollers. There had been time, too, to quell

155

the crippling panic that had started on the phone, and to rehearse some of her lines. She was finally going to give it to the farm-happy cop straight. And the sooner it was over, the better.

But, her little rehearsed "swan song" never got off the ground. Julie slowly backed into her apartment as—in a black turtleneck sweater and tight jeans—Terry charged up to her door.

Talk about fighting walks!

He stormed into the apartment and slammed the door. "Get your purse," he hissed through the one crooked tooth.

"Now, wait just a minute, Terry—"

"I said *get your purse*!"

After another look at his face, Julie obediently went into the bedroom for her bag and a sweater. Moments later she was beside him on the front seat of his old car, heading north on the Outer Drive.

She was grateful for the steamy silence—it gave her time to again collect her thoughts. She could just as easily tell him goodbye on the road—to wherever—as back at her apartment.

When they hit Willow Road, Terry turned west and, much later, onto Route 45. Again they were heading north. In all that time there wasn't a word between them, though several times Julie opened her mouth, each time forgetting her opening line.

They drove through several small towns—Wheeling and Libertyville—with stretches of now-browning open farmland between. Tall silos and squat barns, cattle lazily heading out to pasture, made Julie think of Kansas. Eventually they passed a big wooden sign that said: YOU ARE NOW ENTERING WISCONSIN.

"Now you've done it," she said, looking back at the sign. "Taking me over the state line—that's a *federal* offense."

She thought Terry would give her one of his usual cocky replies, but he only stared straight ahead, his mouth tight as if locked into a line of silent determination.

"Terry, where *are* you taking me?"

"You'll see."

He turned into a long gravel driveway and then pulled up beside a trim, white aluminum-sided farmhouse. He turned off the engine and then, for the first time since they had gotten into the car, he sat back on the seat.

"Well—there it is."

Julie didn't have to ask him what "it" was. *Even got the place picked out.* It was the farm Terry Brannigan hoped to make his own.

When he got out of the car and came around to open her door, Julie sat tightly clutching the purse in her lap, refusing to move an inch. Terry put his hand on her arm and, for a moment, she thought he was going to drag her out of the car.

But the fight slowly went out of his face. "Honey, *please*?"

The owner of the place no doubt had been expecting them. He greeted them warmly at the back door and then went outside himself to let the baby-faced prospective buyer give his blue-jeaned and hair-curlered girl a private tour of the farmhouse.

It was quickly apparent to Julie that the entire place had been completely remodeled. The large parquet-floored kitchen was framed in polished birchwood cabinets, and where the pantry probably had been there was now a cozy café-curtained breakfast nook.

"What do you think?" Terry asked her.

It was breathtakingly beautiful. Any woman would be delirious to have a kitchen like that. Well, *almost* any woman. Julie gave Terry a small shrug as if to say she couldn't care less.

Undaunted by her lack of enthusiasm, Terry took her through the rest of the farmhouse—the pine-paneled front room, the three colorfully papered bedrooms (one obviously a nursery), and even the two bathrooms. The downstairs bathroom still held its original four-footed tub, the owner of the place no doubt being aware of the value of such enamel-coated cast-iron antiques.

"So, what do you think?" Terry asked her again.

But Julie merely gave him that same disinterested shrug. Only this time, it was a bit harder to pull off.

Still determined to give her a complete tour of his intended estate, Terry then led her outside to show her the immediate grounds surrounding the white farmhouse, including the chicken coop, the toolshed and, of course, the somewhat faded red barn.

While the trim, newly-remodeled farmhouse had only faintly reminded Julie of her childhood home back in Kansas, stepping into the musty hay-strewn barn was a sudden leap into her past.

It was not merely nostalgia that suddenly over-whelmed Julie Chambers, but all the agony and ecstasy of adolescence as well. She glanced up to the hayloft—much like the one which served as her own private retreat for shedding the tears that were so much a part of her teens.

She now recalled one especially bitter episode of tears caused by one "town" boy—had she really forgotten his name?—the object of her first real sophomore crush.

Sitting behind her in history class one morning, he had asked, "Doing anything tonight?"

"No—" she had answered, her palms suddenly moist with anticipation.

"Bunch of us are having a hayride tonight. Would you like to come?"

"Well—sure," Julie had said, hoping she hadn't sounded *too* eager.

"Good," said the boy. "We need somebody to pull the wagon."

She had gone home from school that day with a tearful lump in her throat, shedding those bitter, hurtful tears only when she had reached the safety of her father's hayloft.

And perhaps that had been the very day she had created the knight in shining armor who would snatch Julie Chambers up and take her away from it all—the smell of manure, the predawn awakenings, the countless milkings, the tedious egg-candlings, the dreaded weather warnings—all that she hated about life on the farm, including, and perhaps especially, the degrading names that went along with being the farmer's daughter.

"So what do you think?" Terry asked her for the third time as together they walked out of the barn. And when he hopefully looked at her with those honest and vulnerable baby-blue eyes, Julie knew she had to say something.

"The equipment seems to be in good shape, Terry. The barn could use some paint, though." She nodded out toward the open fields. "How many acres?"

"Two-forty."

Compared to her father's acreage back in Kansas, Terry Brannigan's rural enterprise would be more like a mini-farm. But in terms of money today, Julie was sure it was a sizable lump. She didn't ask him how much.

Taking her hand now—the first touch between them since she had gotten out of the car—Terry led her out to survey the fields. It was a long walk as well as an endless series of questions and answers—the future farmer digging for information, and the ex-farm girl doing her best to supply it.

"And what's that?" he asked her for probably the tenth time as, totally walked-out, they both leaned with their arms folded over the rail of a rickety fence. Beyond the fence was a field of still dark and lush green.

"Clover," she told him. "You plant it every other year to put nitrogen back into the soil. Meanwhile, it's good fodder."

"Fodder?"

"Food for the livestock." It was but another instance pointing out Terry Brannigan's total ignorance of farming. She turned and looked at him, his chin resting on his folded arms. "Terry, you don't know the first thing about farming."

"I can *learn.*"

She studied him—the serious glint in his blue eyes, the determined set of his strong Irish-Italian jaw. For the first time since she had met him, Terry Brannigan looked his twenty-eight years.

The sun had long ago slipped behind thick gray clouds and there was a threatening rumble of thunder as they headed for the car. Terry had to switch on the wipers even before they were out of the gravel driveway.

"So what's all this baloney about New York?" he asked after he had turned onto the asphalt highway and they were heading, in a pelt of rain, back south.

"I've been offered a job there."

He turned on the defroster. "Why New York?"

"Why not? There's nothing back here for me."

"You know that isn't true, Julie."

She turned her face to the window. The rain was coming down so hard now she could barely see the harvested cornfield to the right of the road.

"What makes you so dead-set on leaving the force, Terry?"

"I told you."

She was sure he was referring to an earlier conversation in his car, driving home after corned beef and cabbage at his sister's—his remark about policemen seeing things that would straighten her hair.

"I don't believe that, Terry," she now told him. "Your not having the stomach for it anymore, I mean."

He was silent, and she took that as a sign she was right.

"Or that your kids wouldn't be able to find God in the city."

Still no answer.

"You're a good cop, Terry—the world *needs* good cops."

"Yeah," he nodded. "The trick is to keep them alive."

Julie opened her mouth and then quickly closed it. Was *that* what Terry Brannigan didn't have the stomach for—being killed in the line of duty? If so, she could hardly blame him. It gave her a sick feeling in her own stomach to think of him lying in some dark alley in a pool of blood. *Sick* wasn't a strong enough word for it.

"What happened to my sister Julie—I don't want that happening to you."

"To *me*?" As if she hadn't known it all along. As if she hadn't been dreading this very moment.

"Yeah—*you*. Why do you *think* I dragged you out here today?"

Her answer was simply to turn her face to the window again.

With that, Terry suddenly spun the wheel, and the car sharply skidded off into the mud at the side of the road. He switched off the engine.

"Julie, I just asked you to marry me. Do you understand that?"

"Yes—" miserably.

"Well?"

She suddenly burst into tears.

"Julie—I *love* you!"

And that was no surprise, either. He had told her that at least a dozen times when he had so passionately kissed her that morning on her couch. Especially, in the way he had gotten up from that couch and left her apartment before things could get out of hand.

"You'll be number one, Julie. My first—and only."

But she only sat with her face to the window, sobbing. Somehow, she had known that, too. That Terry Brannigan himself was a gem—one of the few guys in the world who didn't think it was just the girl who should be a virgin until her wedding night.

He tried to take her in his arms, but she pulled away.

Terry then sat back on the seat and ran his hand through his rusty hair in obvious frustration. "Julie, I know you feel something for me—I *know* you do."

162

Still sobbing, she nodded.

But, *something*? Had she been *that* successful in masking her true feelings for him—the throb of her heart whenever he touched her, the joy of just being in the same room with him, the agony when she wasn't?

"Then what's wrong?" he demanded.

"I *can't* marry you, Terry."

"*Can't?* What do you mean—*can't*?"

"I just can't."

He was silent a moment, as if mentally sorting through other "dead-end" clues in their relationship, hoping to come up with—or maybe *not* come up with—the right one.

"What then?"

When she didn't answer, he turned and took her by the shoulders, as if to shake the answer from her. "What in heaven's name *is* it?"

"It's *that*!" she sobbed, nodding over her shoulder. "That stupid *farm*!"

They silently sat beside the road as if they might have pulled off merely to sit out the blinding rain. Rather, they were more like two bedside mourners beside the corpse of a dying romance.

"I don't believe it," Terry finally said, shaking his head. "I just don't *believe* it."

He looked over at Julie, quietly sobbing against the rainwashed window.

"I *should* believe it, though. I had a hunch there was something wrong after we went out to Peggy's that night. Everytime I kissed you, I knew you were holding back. If that's the way you felt, why did you wait so long—why didn't you hit me with it that night?"

"I wanted to, Terry—so many times I started to tell you. I guess I was hoping it was all just a pipedream—that you weren't really serious."

"Well, I'm serious."

"I know."

He let out another frustrated sigh. "And just what's so bad about a farm? You were born and raised on one—"

"Yes," she said bitterly, "and hated every minute of it."

"Every minute?" This, skeptically, from Terry.

"All the times I went into town—all those kids calling me hick and hayseed . . ."

"Oh, come on, Julie—" He sounded even more skeptical. "Don't give me that baloney—afraid of somebody calling you a few stupid names."

"Terry, I didn't spend four years in college just to end up back on a farm. I've got a chance now for a decent career."

"Marriage—you don't think *that's* a decent career?"

"I didn't say that."

"You might as well have."

What was he accusing her of? Why did men always resent a woman's wanting a career? Was it because they felt threatened, or was it the male chauvinist inherent in every man? No, she couldn't believe that about Terry Brannigan. He was simply hurting now, trying to strike back in self defense. Not even aware of how much *she* was hurting.

She once again turned her face to the window. *"Terry, I'd die—I'd just wither up and die back on a farm."*

"No, you wouldn't, Julie." He gently turned her

164

face back to his. "Not if you loved me. Not with God's help."

She looked up at him then—at that beautiful tender mouth, forever begging for a kiss. More than anything else in the world, she wanted to give it to him.

But to spend the rest of her life on a farm? She didn't think she could love *any* man that much.

"You've got the wrong girl, Terry."

He took his hand from her face. "Yeah, I guess so."

When Terry pulled up in front of her apartment building, he kept the engine running. Reaching across her, into the glove compartment, he took out a small unopened white envelope. Julie knew it was the one with the hundred dollars in it.

"Here," he said. "I was saving this for a ring. You can give it to your fairy godfather Monday, after he bails you out."

With a squeal of threadbare tires, the jilted cop tore away from the curb as if bent on getting a ticket.

CHAPTER 13

THE RAIN CONTINUED the rest of that day, as if the world might be weeping right along with Julie Chambers.

Having tearfully begun some preliminary packing for her big move, by six o'clock she was almost out of tissues—before she had even half emptied her front room of the pictures and pottery with which she had randomly cluttered it, hoping to make the apartment look homey.

But, despite all her interior decorating with what she called her own private "Julie-junk," the big furnished apartment had never felt anything like home. And maybe that was just it—the fact that the place had come already furnished and none of those furnishings were her own.

If they had been, Julie certainly would not have chosen those stiff and formal beige brocade drapes. They would have been pert, brightly-colored paisley print cafés, with a bouncy valance short enough to let the sunlight through and give her an unfettered view of the lake.

Nor would she have chosen the modern straight-lined sectional sofa upholstered in that dull cocoa brown. It would have been one of those well-padded Early American couches like her mother's, back on the farm. A matching wing-backed chair would be there, too—the kind that enfolded you like the arms of a good friend.

Maybe that was what had always been missing—someone with whom to truly share the apartment. Even with her series of roommates, it had never been sharing, merely co-existing under the same roof. The only time she had felt any real warmth—as if the place might really be lived in—was the morning when she had awakened to the sound of Terry's inept attempts to make breakfast in the kitchen. And, later on the couch, when he had so hungrily kissed her.

O Lord . . .

A fresh flood of tears made Julie abruptly abandon her front room packing to run into the bedroom where she wouldn't have to look at that couch.

There, she found another box of tissues beside her alarm clock. She glumly eyed the small clock, thinking maybe she ought to pack that, too. No, she would still need it to make sure she got to the library Monday, ahead of the bulldozers.

Suddenly Julie thought of another clock she hadn't remembered to pack—her *cuckoo clock*—still up on the wall of the children's reading room! She had been in such a rush to get to the airport the day of her Florida flight, she had completely forgotten the clock upstairs at the library.

To go back for it now, in such torrential rain, would

be madness. She would ask Bill Whittaker to take her over to the library tomorrow, before they went to his classmate's Sunday afternoon wedding.

"This little affair almost didn't come off," said Bill the next day, behind the wheel of his own blue Ford. Splashing through glistening rain puddles, they were heading north on Lake Shore Drive.

"How's that?" said Julie.

When they turned off onto Willow Road, she was sorely aware that this was the very route Terry had taken yesterday when they had driven out to the farm.

"For a while it looked like they might have to elope."

"Why?"

"A big hassle between their parents." Bill reached into his breast pocket for a cigarette and then lit it with the dashboard lighter. "Who was going to pay for what. They decided to split it down the middle."

"Oh." *Money*. Not whether the couple was suited or even ready for something as important as marriage.

"Now with me—" he said, blowing a cloud of smoke in her direction, "there'd never be such a problem."

Rolling down her window in an attempt to let out some of the smoke, Julie wondered if he meant that he didn't have any parents or that he never intended to get married.

She realized then how little she knew about Bill Whittaker, his family background, or his spiritual beliefs—if he had any. Until today, he certainly had never asked her to go to church with him. He seemed amused, now, at the couple's chosen site for their wedding—the popular Chapel-in-the-Woods.

"I haven't been inside a church since the day I ripped off the poor box."

He finally rolled down his window because Julie had begun coughing in the smoke-filled car. She might have openly complained about the damage to both of their lungs if he hadn't raised the more important issue of the salvation of his immortal soul.

"But surely, you *do* believe in God?"

"Oh, sure." He crushed the cigarette out in the ashtray under the dashboard. "I know there's Somebody—Something—out there making it all hang together, the sun and the moon and the stars. Probably got the surprise of His life when those astronauts came so close to knocking on those pearly gates."

"I mean for yourself," said Julie. "Doesn't He mean anything to you—personally?"

He shrugged. "Why should He? He's never done anything for me."

"How can you *say* that? Who do you think gives you the very power to *breathe*?"

"I never asked to be born," Bill answered her. "If the Guy upstairs wants to keep pumping air into me—that's His business. But as long as I'm here, I'm going to grab all I can. And I don't need His or anybody else's help to do it."

And there it is, thought Julie, *the Great American "Me" Gospel according to TV*.

"And just what is it you're so anxious to grab?" she persisted.

"The only things that matter. Money, power, prestige—" He glanced over at her, "—and some cute little chick to enjoy all those goodies with me."

How sad, Julie thought. This was the philosophy

Bill Whittaker would take not only into a marriage—if he even bothered getting married—but into the courtroom, as well. She was wondering how she could possibly answer him, when he saved her the trouble by sharply swerving, through a puddle, into a small asphalt parking lot beside the chapel.

Inside, Julie caught her breath at the simple rustic charm of the quaint A-frame building, much like the roadside chapel where she and her parents had worshipped on the way to Cocoa Beach. Behind the altar, a single gigantic stained-glass window threw a mellow triangle of muted rainbow colors over the rows of wooden pews.

Soft organ music floated over the heads of those already in the pews, a pianissimo accompaniment to the straggle of latecomers softly padding down the blue-carpeted aisle, carefully avoiding the white runner laid down for the bride's final steps as a single woman.

Bill led Julie down the aisle to one of the front pews on the right, to take their place among the whispering collection of friends of the groom.

Now a hush fell over the little chapel as the organist paused before breaking into the strains of Lohengrin's Wedding March. Julie turned, with the other guests, to watch the small procession. First came the maid of honor, a petite, pale blonde in a teal chiffon gown; then Reno Fanelli's bride—breathtakingly beautiful in white Chantilly lace—on the arm of her father. Julie missed the even smaller procession of two, from the room just off the sanctuary to the front of the chapel.

When she turned back to the altar, Julie again caught her breath. She immediately recognized the groom as one of her book-hauling partners the night of

Operation Sidewalk. What made her catch her breath, though, was shifting her gaze to the groom's best man to stare directly into the eyes of Terry Brannigan, resplendent in a pale blue tuxedo.

Nice going, Dumbo . . . Fanelli's the cop's cousin.

"What's the matter?" Bill whispered as Julie slumped back against the wooden seat. And then he himself looked toward the altar and gave a contemptuous snort.

"I hope this little circus is over soon," he said under his breath, "before I get sick."

When she finally crept between the sheets that night, Julie was willing to accept Bill's description of the wedding as a wake. She had died a thousand small deaths before arriving home.

After the five o'clock ceremony, the entire congregation had driven over to the nearby Country Barn for a sit-down dinner and buffet "sweets table" in a private banquet room behind the quaintly decorated barn-turned-roadside-restaurant.

It might not have been so bad if Bill hadn't kept slipping away from their table to join his fellow "mourners" at the dimly lit bar in the main restaurant.

Apparently he thought it was perfectly all right to leave her alone, as long as he occasionally ambled back to bring her a fresh ginger ale. Besides, she had twice refused to join him at the bar.

As it was, Julie spent most of the evening chatting with the middle-aged couple across the table from her, trying to keep her eyes from the head table—and one particular blue-tuxedoed member of the wedding party.

Seeing him and his partner in the reception line had been bad enough. The pale little blonde had clung to his arm, her face glowing as if might be *her* wedding day.

And every other time Julie had glanced their way, the maid of honor had still been clinging to Reno Fanelli's gorgeous best man. As if—like those flying Florida lovebugs—they had been stuck together with super glue when she had met him at the altar.

On his final return to their table, Bill Whittaker actually sat down beside Julie. And—getting a good whiff of his breath—she fervently wished that he hadn't.

"What's with you and Brannigan?" he asked, nodding toward the head table.

"That's all over." Inwardly, she winced at the pain of actually putting it into words.

"Good." He casually draped his arm over the back of her chair. "Probably the smartest thing you did in your whole life."

Fingering the fresh glass of ginger ale he had brought her, Julie remained silent.

"What can a cop offer a girl," said Bill, "except long, lonely nights and a stack of unpaid bills?"

But he won't be a cop much longer, she thought ruefully. *He'll soon be forking hay in his own barn.*

"Now you take a promising young attorney," Bill suggested. "He makes the right connections . . . In two or three years he's on Easy Street."

When Julie gave him no response, Bill pulled his chair closer and took her free hand.

"You know what a good lawyer pulls in each year?"

"No," she said dully.

"Enough to give his wife just about anything—a big house, expensive furs, even her own private library, if that's what she wants."

Julie made no comment, torturing herself with yet another glance at the head table. She was immediately sorry. Because now—with the best man and maid of honor apparently sharing a good joke—it was hard to tell just who was clinging to whom.

"Look," persisted Bill, "what I'm saying now, Julie—my asking you out tonight—has nothing to do with Fowler. Sure, maybe it didn't start out that way, but now it's just you and me. I'm crazy about you, Julie."

"What?" she asked half-heartedly.

"I just told you I'm in love with you. I want you to marry me."

"Oh."

"Is that all you can say—*oh*?"

It was a struggle, but Julie finally took her eyes from the other couple, focusing them on her own partner, trying to recall exactly what he had just said. Something about being in love with her.

"I'm sorry, Bill." She took her hand from his. "I'm sorry you think you're in love with me, because I don't feel the same way about you."

Now it was his turn to fall silent.

"Honestly, Bill," she looked directly into his eyes. "I *am* sorry."

"Whoopie," he said, turning away. "*You're* sorry, *I'm* sorry, Fanelli's going to be sorry—this *must* be a wake." With that, he got up from the table and headed back to the bar.

And before Fanelli's bride was ready to toss her bouquet, Bill Whittaker was so bombed that one of his classmates had to drive Julie home.

Tears. How many could a person cry? Was one born with just so many and, when they were all used up, it would never be possible to cry again?

In the privacy of her darkened bedroom, Julie poured into her pillow the torrent of tears she had been holding back since she had first seen Terry Brannigan at the altar.

Why had God allowed them to meet if it was to end like this? Was it to give Julie Chambers a share in Christ's suffering—a cross she would carry the rest of her life? Would the sound of the squad car, the sight of a blue uniform, forever be a lance in her own heart?

Sobbing into her pillow, Julie suffered her own private agony, recalling all the times she and Terry had gone to Steiner's *Sommergarten*—that last time, when he had guilelessly asked her if she was "his girl."

O Lord . . .

She also relived the agony of yesterday, the rain beating down on the roof of his old car and how—with curlers still in her hair—she so desperately had wanted to kiss him.

Lord . . .

And tonight! Terry Brannigan, with another girl on his arm!

Lord . . . it hurts so much!

But wasn't it her own fault? Hadn't she sensed from the start that Terry Brannigan spelled heartbreak? Yet, hadn't she let herself fall hopelessly in love with him?

Couldn't she have spared herself all this agony? Once she had known about the farm, shouldn't she have told him what she so painfully had had to tell him yesterday, in the rain: "You've got the wrong girl, Terry."

And *wasn't* she the wrong girl? Didn't Terry Brannigan need a woman who would love him so much it wouldn't matter *where* they lived—*what* he might do for a living?

Terry, I'd die—I'd just wither up and die back on a farm . . .

No, you wouldn't Julie—not if you loved me.

Suddenly the memory of another rainy day washed over her—her last full day in Florida. And she recalled what Ellen Jackson had said to her down on the beach before they finally parted.

"Someday you'll have to tell me *your* story—about how you met *him*."

"Who?"

"That policeman you're so crazy about."

Julie had opened her mouth as if to object, but Ellen had gently closed it with a suntanned finger. "It's not only on every page of that last story, Julie—it's written all over your face."

She had then taken Julie by the chin and raised her suddenly tearful dark eyes to hers.

"Julie, if you love the guy *that* much, don't let *anything* stand in the way. With your love—and God's—I'm sure it will all work out."

God's love? Just his everyday boundless love—or some special outpouring? For wouldn't it take some kind of "miracle" for her to again willingly live with the ever-present smell of manure, the muddy boots, the hayseed in his hair? A miracle to help her endure the rural isolation, those harsh early-morning risings, those bleak winter nights?

And what of her writing?

Was that God-given talent to be buried under a mound of hay while she struggled to keep the farmer's house clean, candle his eggs, preserve his pickles, and cheer him up when his crop failed?

On, come on, Julie, a small voice chided her, *if you could write children's stories on a smelly Chicago bus, you could write an epic in a nice, cozy café-curtained breakfast nook!*

Wasn't that true? Might not a literary candle as freely shine from a remodeled Wisconsin farmhouse as from an editor's desk in New York City? Indeed, might it not shine all the more brightly—its timid flame fed by the breath of true Christian love? Wouldn't Terry's belief in her as a writer only spur her on to becoming an even better one?

Without a doubt. But if she believed this, why had she used her talent—the claim of a decent career—in turning Terry down? Was she, after all, a feminist misfit, denying her God-ordained role in life?

God's mysterious ways . . . the Lord's will . . .

Weren't those words just pious camouflage for Julie Chambers's own self-centered will? Wasn't she merely running from what God had intended she should be, a wife and mother?

No. She loved children.

And, though they weren't even born yet, she already loved Terry Brannigan's red-haired, freckle-nosed little imps. Almost as much as she loved him.

Julie suddenly clutched her tear-dampened pillow, giving it all the fierce hugs she had denied the only man she would ever love.

"*Oh, Terry. . . .*"

She buried her face in the damp, lifeless pillow.

Jesus, help me . . . tell me what you want me to do!

Before falling into exhausted sleep, Julie remembered something she desperately wished to forget:

Terry Brannigan's hungry kiss that morning on the couch.

And the most soulful and heart-wrenching of all his true confessions: "I *need* you, Julie. I *love* you."

CHAPTER 14

THE MORNING SUN BRIGHT ON THE TUFTS of her white heirloom bedspread made Julie think of those orthopedic mattress commercials in which the sleep-refreshed girl joyously springs out of bed. But, waking with a still-damp pillow and a throbbing headache, Julie doubted she could even crawl out of her bed.

Groaning, she slowly rolled over on her side— away from the window—wishing she had remembered to draw the shade last night. Conscious only of her pounding head, it was some time before she realized the sun was much too bright for that time of day. She got up on one elbow and looked at the alarm clock on her nightstand.

Eleven o'clock! It *couldn't* be!

Twelve minutes later—minus her usual morning shower and cup of coffee—Julie was down on the street, climbing into a waiting cab.

It would cost her a small fortune, but she didn't care. Breathlessly, she told the driver her destination—two stops, actually—and then slumped back in the rear seat of the cab, praying it wasn't too late; groaning at every red light—ten of them before they even hit Lake Shore Drive; wanting to scream as the taxi waited—meter merrily ticking away—for the Michigan Avenue bridge to come back down.

Just as maddening was the jam of noontime traffic on Wacker Drive, and finding the street in front of the library already barricaded. She had to leave the cab and run the last two blocks, praying she was not too late, but certain the wrecking crew had not been. At the end of her breathless run, she found she was right. The street was swarming with hired mercenaries, not a truly human face in the entire helmeted squad.

Bent on her own private mission, Julie completely missed a number of other very human and very happy dark faces. If she *had* noticed them, she surely would have wondered at all those smiles. And she might have heard what the children were crying out to her— in both English and Spanish—as she pushed through the crowd. What Maria Sanchez and three other Latino women were trying to tell her as she passed by them:

"Gracias a Dios!"
"Que dia alegre!"
"Ellos se lo llevado!"
"La casa bonita esta salvado!"

Not hearing them at all, Julie continued pushing through the crowd until she reached what should have been the wrought-iron gateway to Kevin McDonough's mansion. Her heart sank as she saw the two giant stone stanchions flat on the grass, as if torn from their cement moorings by a tornado.

Slowly she raised her eyes to look at the mansion

179

itself and then found herself breathing another prayer. *Thank You, Lord!* Though half the foundation was already gone, the old red-brick "castle" still stood.

And then she saw it parked on the grass to the side of the house—a white TV truck. Its troop of ear-plugged cameramen scurried about the lawn with their portable scanners over their shoulders—each focusing on a different, perhaps more interesting shot.

There was another man—this one with only a microphone—sitting on the still-intact steps of the doomed library. He stood up as Julie came up the stone steps.

"You the librarian?"

"Yes, but—"

"Hey, fellas—*over here!*"

Two of the cameramen immediately came sprinting over.

"This is the babe," said the guy with the microphone.

"Stay right where you are," said one of the cameramen, adjusting his lens. "Yeah, that's a good shot—you on the stairs."

"Look," said Julie, "this is ridiculous. I'm not here to—"

"That's good," said the cameraman. "Keep your hand on the railing. Now smile."

"*Smile!* " she said incredulously. "You expect me to *smile?*"

The man with the microphone stared at Julie as if *she* were the one who was now being totally ridiculous. "What are you—some kind of *nut?*"

"Sure. I go out of my mind every time they tear down a library."

"You mean—you *don't know?*"

"Know what?"

He again looked at her in amazement. Then he slowly broke into a grin. "Hey—that's an even *better* angle!" He turned to his colleagues with their ready-to-shoot cameras. "The little chick doesn't even *know!*"

At that, the cameras immediately began turning, as if their operators might be filming the scoop of the year. Julie almost felt sorry for them, knowing she was about to burst their little bubble.

"You may as well *all* know," she said, unable to avoid the microphone suddenly thrust into her face. "I only came for my clock."

"Beautiful, beautiful—" whispered one of the cameramen, as if the library steps were a stage and he was coaching her from the wings.

"My cuckoo clock."

Not only did that little unrehearsed line go into the TV microphone, but the men's spontaneous loud laugh, as well.

Her cheeks suddenly burning—*What was so funny?*—Julie gave the still-chuckling camera crew what she hoped was the closing line in her impromptu television debut: "I am not going to sit down in front of any bulldozers—in front of *anything.*"

"You don't *need* to," came a familiar voice from behind her.

The cameras suddenly stopped clicking as Paddy Fowler came down the library steps. Apparently the TV newsmen thought they had filmed all the most interesting action—or they were reluctant to give one of the city fathers any free preelection publicity.

Whatever the case, Julie thought the alderman looked somewhat naked without his usual soggy cigar.

"What do you mean—I don't *need* to?" Julie demanded, meaning his comment about her aborted sitdown.

"Just look," said Fowler. He nodded to the helmeted wrecking crew, chipping away at the foundation of the library.

"I'd rather *not* look," she told him.

Fowler then gently took her by the arm as if he were, after all, a member of the human race. "They're not tearing the library down, sweetheart. They're *moving* it."

"*Moving* it!" She stared into the alderman's flushed face. "You're joking."

But this time Bill Whittaker wasn't around to tell her otherwise. His former boss himself had to do it.

"No bunk," said Fowler. "This crew is here to haul the old dump away."

"I don't believe it."

"Well, you'd better. Because I'm pretty sure the city's going to want you to keep running the place— once it's replanted."

"They'll have to find somebody else to do that."

Julie glanced toward the police station—her intended second stop in her emergency cab ride. And then it occurred to her that she had not yet asked the most obvious question.

"But *where?* Where in the world are they *moving* it?"

"Well, now," said Fowler, "just stop and think, Julie. Where *is* the only open piece of land in this ward—other than the playground?"

Her mind again drifting to the police station and her even more important mission there, it took Julie a few moments to think. "The Blue Angel," she finally said. "Steiner's *Sommergarten.*"

182

"Give the little lady a fresh cigar." Meaning, of course, that she had come up with the right answer.

"*Steiner?*" she said incredulously. "Steiner actually sold it to the city?"

"Not Steiner," he said. "The *new* owner. And it didn't cost the city a lousy cent."

"I don't understand."

"It's simple."

But, before he went on to tell her how simple, Fowler loudly sighed. And Julie could almost see his hopes for reelection, his "last hurrah," slowly crumbling on the stone stops.

"Somebody bought the garden this morning and turned it over to the city. With the stipulation, of course, that it was only for the library."

"But *who?*" Julie asked with her hand again on the stone railing, suddenly feeling the need of some support. "Who would want to do a thing like *that?*"

Not only did the Midtown alderman look naked without his cigar, he suddenly also looked much older. And very tired.

"That cop," he said wearily. "That crazy red-headed cop."

Julie ran all the way to the police station. He was there at the desk with his head bent over some papers—just as he had been the very first day she had laid eyes on him.

Breathlessly, she leaned over the counter. "That was the money for the farm, *wasn't* it!"

He said nothing, penciling a note on one of the sheets.

"Terry—those were your *life's savings!*"

"Big deal." He stacked the sheets together, got up and took them over to the filing cabinet.

"Terry—why did you *do* it?"

"Not for anything noble—if *that's* what you want me to say." He opened the top file drawer. "I'm no storybook hero, Julie—just a dumb lovesick cop."

He dropped the sheets into the metal file and then slammed the drawer shut. He stood with his back to her. "I don't want any crummy farm, Julie—not without you."

She burst into tears.

The cop came out from behind his counter and took her in his arms. "Why are you crying? I thought you'd be *happy*. Cinderella not only gets her castle—but Prince Charming, too."

That only made her sob louder.

He nodded toward the library. "Spoiled your grand exit? If it'll do any good, I'll go hire a bulldozer and we can *both* lie down in front of it."

"Oh, stop it, Terry!" She somehow managed to stop crying. "I'm not going *anywhere*. And I wasn't going through with that stupid sitdown, either."

"Yeah? When did you decide that?"

"Last night."

"Why?"

"Because—" and she burst into tears again, "—I didn't think a farmer's wife should have a police record!"

It took some time for that to sink in. And when it did, Julie felt it go through him like a knife—the knowledge of what, in heartsick haste, he had actually done.

"Oh, no!" he groaned. And when he tightly clutched her to him, Julie thought the cop was going to cry.

She still thought so, even when he slowly shook his head.

"Oh, man, that's *funny!*" When he suddenly started laughing, it was the almost hysterical laugh of a man who had just thrown his life's savings down the drain. "That's really *funny!*"

Whatever it was—laughing or really crying—Terry paused only once to again shake his head in disbelief and then start in all over again.

But eventually he stopped. And when he did, he was totally drained. Julie could both hear it and feel it as—with her still in his arms—he slumped back against the counter.

"I would've made a lousy farmer, anyway."

"Oh, darling—"

She wrapped her arms around his neck and all but smothered the world's most beautiful cop, giving him the all-consuming kiss he had so long been begging for.

"Terry, I love you so much—"

"You'd *better.*"

Yes, God works in mysterious ways. Pray for an angel and you get a cop. Yet who was going to argue that Terry Brannigan wasn't an angel?

Certainly not Julie Chambers. Certainly not while he was kissing her.

ABOUT THE AUTHOR

MARY LAPIETRA describes herself as an "incurable romantic." Although THE DISGUISE OF LOVE is her first adult novel, she is the author of eight children's books and three award-winning children's plays.

She has done public relations work for the City of Northlake, the Northlake Public Library, and the Northlake Community Theatre. Her husband, Vince, is also active in community affairs, currently serving a second term as 4th Ward Alderman for the City of Northlake.

One of eleven children—born and raised in Chicago—Mary is the mother of four and grandmother of three. She lives with her husband and two sons in Northlake, a suburb of the "Windy City."

A Letter To Our Readers

Dear Reader:

Pioneering is an exhilarating experience, filled with opportunities for exploring new frontiers. The Zondervan Corporation is proud to be the first major publisher to launch a series of inspirational romances designed to inspire and uplift as well as to provide wholesome entertainment. In order that we might better contribute to your reading enjoyment, we would appreciate your taking a few minutes to respond to the following questions and return to:

> Anne Severance, Editor
> The Zondervan Publishing House
> 1415 Lake Drive, S.E.
> Grand Rapids, Michigan   49506

1. Did you enjoy reading THE DISGUISE OF LOVE?
   - ☐ Very much. I would like to see more books by this author!
   - ☐ Moderately
   - ☐ I would have enjoyed it more if _____

2. Where did you purchase this book? _____

3. What influenced your decision to purchase this book?
   - ☐ Cover   ☐ Back cover copy
   - ☐ Title   ☐ Friends
   - ☐ Publicity   ☐ Other _____

4. Please rate the following elements from 1 (poor) to 10 (superior).

   ☐ Heroine   ☐ Plot
   ☐ Hero   ☐ Inspirational theme
   ☐ Setting   ☐ Secondary characters

5. Which settings would you like to see in future Serenade/Saga Books?

   _____ _____

   _____ _____

6. What are some inspirational themes you would like to see treated in future books?

   _____ _____

   _____ _____

7. Would you be interested in reading other Serenade/Serenata or Serenade/Saga Books?

   ☐ Very interested
   ☐ Moderately interested
   ☐ Not interested

8. Please indicate your age range:

   ☐ Under 18   ☐ 25–34   ☐ 46–55
   ☐ 18–24   ☐ 35–45   ☐ Over 55

9. Would you be interested in a Serenade book club? If so, please give us your name and address:

   Name _____

   Occupation _____

   Address _____

   City _____ State _____ Zip _____

Serenade Saga Books are inspirational romances in historical settings, designed to bring you the American saga of faith and love.

Serenade Saga books available in your local bookstore:

#1 SUMMER SNOW, Sandy Dengler
#2 CALL HER BLESSED, Jeanette Gilge
#3 INA, Karen Baker Kletzing
#4 JULIANA OF CLOVER HILL,
     Brenda Knight Graham
#5 SONG OF THE NEREIDS, Sandy Dengler
#6 ANNA'S ROCKING CHAIR,
     Elaine Watson
#7 IN LOVE'S OWN TIME,
     Susan C. Feldhake
#8 YANKEE BRIDE, Jane Peart
#9 LIGHT OF MY HEART, Kathleen Karr
#10 LOVE BEYOND SURRENDER,
     Susan C. Feldhake
#11 ALL THE DAYS AFTER SUNDAY,
     Jeanette Gilge
#12 WINTERSPRING, Sandy Dengler
#13 HAND ME DOWN THE DAWN,
     Mary Harwell Sayler
#14 REBEL BRIDE, Jane Peart
#15 SPEAK SOFTLY, LOVE, Kathleen Yapp
#16 FROM THIS DAY FORWARD, Kathleen Karr
#17 THE RIVER BETWEEN, Jacquelyn Cook
#18 VALIANT BRIDE, Jane Peart
#19 WAIT FOR THE SUN, Maryn Langer
#20 KINCAID OF CRIPPLE CREEK, Peggy Darty

Watch for other books in the *Serenade Saga* series coming soon: